Anne Stuart
Falling Angel

The RITA represents the highest award of excellence
in the romance industry. It is presented annually by
the Romance Writers of America to the authors of
the year's best romance novels in eleven categories
at an awards ceremony during the RWA's national
conference. This year, eight hundred romance novels
competed for the coveted awards.

Anne Stuart received this award for *Falling Angel*.

"You're asking for trouble, Carrie."

Gabriel spoke softly, knowing if he touched her his fate was sealed for eternity....

"I know," she whispered.

He told himself to move, to push past her and walk out of her house. What was the saying? Damned if you do, damned if you don't? Oh, Gabriel Falconi was damned all right. There'd be no heaven for the likes of him....

"Carrie," he whispered again. As he reached out to cup her pale face, his thumbs brushing against her trembling lips, he knew that in this moment—the moment his hands had touched her—there could be no turning back....

ANNE STUART

FALLING ANGEL

Harlequin Books

TORONTO • NEW YORK • LONDON
AMSTERDAM • PARIS • SYDNEY • HAMBURG
STOCKHOLM • ATHENS • TOKYO • MILAN
MADRID • WARSAW • BUDAPEST • AUCKLAND

ISBN 0-373-60073-9

FALLING ANGEL

Dear Reader,

Step into the WINNER'S CIRCLE, with a set of special romance novels guaranteed to win your heart!

In this outstanding selection of Harlequin and Silhouette books, we've chosen to showcase award-winners, those novels that professional lovers of romance are always talking about, and readers can never forget. Some of your favorite authors have contributed their works to this collection, including Anne Stuart, Penny Jordan, Curtiss Ann Matlock, Dallas Schulze, Kathleen Korbel and Glenda Sanders.

Look for the WINNER'S CIRCLE insignia on a new title each month from January to June, and you'll know you've picked a winner!

Happy reading...

The Editors of Harlequin and Silhouette books

Prologue

"This isn't working out, Mr. MacVey."

Emerson Wyatt MacVey III looked up and blinked. The light was blinding up there, endless bright white light set against a clear crystal blue. It gave him a headache. "Could you be more specific?" He managed to make his voice coolly polite.

The woman standing in front of him was an impressive figure, and he didn't like to be impressed. She was ageless, of course, with smooth, unlined skin, pure white hair, a long, slender body and large hands. She was possessed of the most frightening eyes he'd ever seen. Large, dark, powerful, they looked right through you, seeing everything you wanted to keep hidden.

Not that he needed to keep anything hidden, he reminded himself. He'd lived his life as he'd seen fit, and he didn't need to make excuses to anyone.

"How long have you been here?" the woman asked in a voice even colder than his. Augusta, that was her name. It suited her.

Emerson shook his head. "I don't remember. Time moves differently..."

"Then I'll jog your memory. You've been here for seventeen months, Mr. MacVey. And you've shown very little improvement."

"Seventeen months?" he echoed, shocked out of his determined cool. "It was only three months yesterday."

"As you've said, time passes a little differently up here," Augusta said sternly. "You've been dead for seventeen months, Mr. MacVey. And you're still the same arrogant, argumentative person you were when you arrived."

He tipped back in his chair, staring up at her. "Yeah? Well, maybe I wasn't ready to die. You ever consider that? Maybe thirty-two years old was a little young to have a massive heart attack. Maybe someone made a mistake, pulled me out a little too early."

"You've seen too many movies. We don't make mistakes."

"Then why am I here?" Frustration was building, ready to spill over. "Why aren't I floating around with the angels, playing the harp and all that crap?"

"You are an angel, Mr. MacVey."

That stopped him for a moment. He glanced down at himself. Same body, thin, patrician. Same English wool three-piece suit that he died in. It had been ripped off him when the medics had labored over him, trying to bring him back. Fortunately he'd been able to repair the damage. "Really? Then why don't I have pearly wings and a halo?"

Augusta smiled sourly, and suddenly she reminded him of his maternal grandmother, a cold-blooded old tartar who'd managed to terrorize three presidents, a prime minister and her only grandson quite effectively. "Your status is in no way assured, Mr. MacVey. There are two choices. Heaven, or the other place. We're not certain where you fit."

When he'd had his heart attack it had been a huge explosion of red-hot pain. This was cold, icy cold, and even more frightening. "What do you mean by that?" His voice stumbled slightly, and he cursed himself for showing weakness. Augusta wouldn't respect weakness, any more than his grandmother would.

"I mean that you need to earn your place up here. On earth you were petty, grasping, cold and heartless. All you cared about was making money and amassing possessions. Where are your possessions now, Mr. MacVey?"

"It's a little too late to do anything about that, isn't it?" He managed to muster a trace of defiance.

"On the contrary. It's not too late at all. You're going to be given a second chance. One month, to be exact. You're going back to earth and try to right some of the wrongs you've done. If you prove yourself worthy of redemption then you'll be allowed to move on. If you fail . . ." She made a desultory gesture.

"The other place?" Emerson supplied.

"Exactly." Her voice was sepulchral.

Emerson controlled his instinctive start of panic. He didn't want to go to hell. It was just that simple. But not simple enough that he wasn't ready to put up an argument. "Won't people find it a little surprising to see me running around again? I imagine they had a full-blown funeral, people weeping and all that."

"No one wept."

Again that stinging cold sharpness where his damaged heart should be. "Don't be ridiculous. People always cry at funerals."

"No one cried at yours. But then, not very many people showed up for it, either. Only one person cried for you, Mr. MacVey. And it was one of the people whose lives your selfishness destroyed."

He racked his brain for people he might have injured, people he might have destroyed, but he came up with a comforting blank. "I didn't destroy anyone."

"Oh, you didn't set out to do so, I grant you that. In a way, that almost makes it worse. Does the name Caroline Alexander mean anything to you?"

"Not a thing."

"She was your secretary for three months."

He shrugged. "I went through a lot of secretaries."

"You certainly went through Carrie. You fired her on a whim, Mr. MacVey, on Christmas Eve, and that started a chain of events that totally devastated her life. She's one of your projects. You have to fix what you so callously destroyed."

"And how am I supposed to do that? I don't imagine she'd want me anywhere near her."

"You aren't going back as Emerson Wyatt MacVey III. Things aren't going to be quite so easy this time around. You'll have your work cut out for you. You have three lives to save, MacVey. And you'll have one month to do it. You go back on Thanksgiving. And you return on Christmas Eve. We'll decide then whether you've earned your right to move on."

"But..."

"Don't fret, Mr. MacVey," Augusta said. "You won't be going alone. You'll have a little help. An observer, so to speak. Someone to keep an eye on you, make sure you're not making things even worse. I don't have a great deal of faith in this particular experiment. I think you're a lost cause, but I've been overruled in this matter.''

Thank heaven for small favors, Emerson thought.

''Not a small favor at all,'' Augusta replied, reading his thoughts with an ease he could never get accustomed to. ''You will go back to earth and repair some of the damage you have caused, or you will be doomed to the other place. And you won't like it, MacVey. You won't like it at all.''

He had no doubt of that. ''What exactly am I supposed to do?''

Augusta smiled, exposing very large, very yellow teeth. ''You will fix Carrie Alexander's life, which, I warn you, is no small task. And you must find two other people you've harmed, and somehow make amends.''

''How am I supposed to find two people I've harmed?'' he demanded indignantly.

''The problem, MacVey, won't be in finding people you've harmed. The problem will be in finding people you haven't hurt during your tenure on earth. Good luck,'' she said sourly. ''You'll need it.''

''But what about my observer? You said I was going to have some help,'' he said, no longer bothering to disguise the panic in his voice.

''We don't want to make it too easy on you, MacVey,'' Augusta said with saccharine sweetness. ''You'll find out who your observer is in good time. As a matter of fact, no one's offered to take on the task. They all think you're a lost cause.''

Emerson sat up a little straighter. He was a man who was used to challenges, would do just about anything to triumph over impossible odds. "Want to bet?"

"We don't gamble up here, Mr. MacVey."

"You just pass judgment."

"Exactly."

"Great," he muttered under his breath, despising the old woman almost as much as he'd despised his grandmother. "So you're going to dump me back on earth and the rest is up to me?"

"That about sums it up. Oh, and you'll be given a slight edge. Miracles, Mr. MacVey. You'll be given the opportunity to perform three miracles. How and when you choose to use that particular gift will be up to you. But you cannot use more than one per person."

"Great," he said again. "Any other rules?"

"You're not to tell anyone who you are. But you needn't worry about that—you won't be able to."

"What do you mean by that?"

"You'll find out. Are you ready?"

"Ready? Last time I looked it was August."

"It's late November. Thanksgiving, to be exact. Time to go."

"But..."

"No more questions, Mr. MacVey. You're on your own."

The light grew sharper, clearer, brighter still, until it felt as if his head were about to explode. The cold stinging in his chest was like a stiletto-sharp knife, a column of ice that speared through his body until it began to dissolve into a thousand tiny crystals. And then he was gone, cast out, drifting through the black night like the flakes of snow surrounding him, no two ever the same. And all was black.

Chapter One

He squinted at the swirling white light in front of him, trying to orient himself. He was cold, his feet, his hands, even the tip of his nose was cold. It took him a moment to realize the bright, fuzzy light in front of him was the headlights from the vehicle he was driving. It was snowing, heavily, and the light barely penetrated the thick darkness.

"Damn," he said out loud, he wasn't quite sure why. Maybe he wanted to hear the sound of his own voice, to prove he was alive.

Except that he wasn't alive. He'd been dead of a massive heart attack for almost two years now. And it wasn't the sound of his own voice coming from his throat.

He dropped his gaze, from the storm beyond his windshield, to his hands clutching the steering wheel. They weren't his hands. His hands were on the small side, neat, perfectly manicured, slightly soft. The hands in front of him were big hands, with long, slender fingers, short nails, calluses and scars marring the skin. They were the hands of a working man. Not the hands of a man who'd never done anything more strenuous than use the carefully padded equipment at his upscale health club.

"Damn," he said again, testing the sound. Lower than his voice. With a slight huskiness in it. No discernible accent. That was something at least. What the hell had Augusta done to him?

He glanced up in the rearview mirror, but all he could see was the swirling darkness behind him. He shifted it, angling his head to get a look at his face. And promptly drove off the snow-slick road into a ditch, banging his head against the windshield.

The engine stalled, the headlight spearing into the darkness. He hadn't been wearing a seat belt. How strange. He always wore a seat belt. Of course, in New York, where he'd lived, it had been the law, and he'd been a very law-abiding citizen. But he'd been wearing seat belts since he'd first ridden in a car. And what use had they done him? he thought bitterly. Seat belts weren't much good against a heart attack.

He jerked the mirror down, almost ripping it from its mooring in the tattered roof of the pickup truck he'd been driving, and stared down. It was no wonder he'd driven off the road. A total stranger stared back at him.

Emerson Wyatt MacVey III had been a compact, good-looking yuppie, with perfectly styled sandy blond hair, even features, clear-framed glasses and carefully orthodontured teeth. He'd had icy blue eyes, and a faintly supercilious expression on his naturally pale face.

The man who stared back at him was his exact opposite in every way. Dark brown, almost black, eyes, long, curling black hair that obviously hadn't been cut in months, a high forehead, high cheekbones, a large, sensual-looking mouth, and a strong Roman nose all composed a face that didn't belong in his world.

He glanced down at the long, jeans-clad legs, the faded flannel shirt beneath the down vest, the big, strong hands that had first startled him. Whatever he had become, it was as different from Emerson MacVey as night and day.

Enough of his ingrained nature remained that he carefully turned off the truck lights, pulled the key from the ignition and locked the truck when he climbed out into the mini blizzard. A stray thought hit him—who would steal an old truck from a ditch in the middle of a blinding snowstorm?—but he ignored that. Emerson was a man who locked his car. Even if he was currently possessed of an old pickup that looked as if it belonged in a junkyard, it was still his car, his possession, and he wasn't going to let anyone else make off with it. Who knew what else this stranger possessed?

He could see lights in the distance, through the swirl of snow. He shivered as a mantle of snow covered him, and he stared down at his feet. Way down, and the feet were big, like his hands. And wearing only sneakers to wade through the drifts.

He shivered again, grimaced, and then struck out toward the lights. He felt a little dizzy, and he realized there was a throbbing where he'd smashed his head against the windshield. He touched it gingerly, and beneath the melting snow he could feel a respectable lump. Maybe that could explain away some of his confusion when he asked for help from whoever lived nearby. Because he sure as hell felt confused.

As he drew nearer, he saw it was an old farmhouse, in about as good condition as the truck he'd been driving. The front porch sagged, the windows had sheets of plastic stapled around them, rather than decent triple-track storm windows, and ripped tar paper had been tacked around the bottom of the house. He imagined that the roof was in equally shoddy condition beneath the thick blanket of snow. He could smell the rich, aromatic scent of wood smoke, and he stopped still. In his endless, timeless sojourn at the Waystation he'd been able to see and hear and even feel things. But there hadn't been anything to smell.

He took another deep sniff. Turkey. Roast turkey, and the faint trace of cinnamon and apples. And he remembered with a start what Augusta had told him. He was coming back on Thanksgiving, leaving on Christmas Eve. It was Thanksgiving, and someone was just sitting down to dinner.

And he was standing outside in a blowing snowstorm, freezing to death. He shook himself, running a hand through his long, thick hair in a gesture that was both foreign and automatic. And he stepped up to the ancient, scarred door and rapped.

In a moment the door was flung open, letting out a flood of warmth and light and noise. Someone was standing there, silhouetted against the brightness, and he could make out the slender shape of a woman. Beyond her were others, various shapes and sizes, friendly, nosy, he thought, swaying slightly.

"My truck's gone off the road," he said, then fell silent, shocked once more at the unfamiliar sound of his new voice. Deeper than his old one. Slower. "Can I use your phone?"

She moved toward him, reaching for him, hands touching his snow-covered sleeve, and he realized he hadn't been touched. Not since all those technicians had labored over him. And even then he hadn't felt it. He'd been a few steps back, watching them as they tried to save him.

"You must be frozen," she said in a voice that was light, musical, oddly charming. "Come in out of the storm and we'll warm you up. It won't do you any good to call anyone at this hour. Steve runs the only garage in town, and he's gone to his mother's for Thanksgiving. But there are a bunch of us here, we'll get you out."

He let her pull him into the kitchen, into the noise and warmth and hubbub, even as he wanted to pull back. It hurt in there. The bright light hurt his eyes, accustomed to the darkness. The friendly conversation hurt his ears, accustomed to silence. The heat hurt his skin, which had grown so cold, so very cold. It was life, he realized. For the first time in months, no, years, he was no longer dead, no longer in a cool, sullen cocoon, and the shock of it was intensely painful.

He turned to look at his hostess, the woman who'd pulled him into the kitchen, and got his second shock of the night. This time it wasn't a stranger's eyes he stared into. It was the warm blue-eyed gaze of a woman who'd once spent three thankless months as his incompetent secretary. It was Carrie Alexander, one of the people he'd come to save.

She looked the same, and yet different, somehow. She'd always been thin, a dancer, he thought he remembered. But now she was even leaner, almost skinny, and there were faint shadows behind her smil-

ing eyes. And then she was no longer smiling, as a
frown washed over her face, and he wondered for a
moment whether she'd recognized him.

"You've been hurt," she said, reaching up, way up,
to push his hair away from his face. He tried to jerk
back, but she wouldn't let him, and her fingers on his
chilled skin were warm and incredibly gentle. "You
must have hit your head when you went off the road.
Let me do something about that while Maggie gets you
a cup of coffee to warm you up."

"Please..." he said, and wondered where that word
came from. He'd never considered it an essential part
of his vocabulary. "I just need to get my truck out of
the ditch."

"Jeffie and I will help you."

A man stepped forward, a huge, lumbering bear of
a man, except that for some reason his eyes weren't
quite on a level with Emerson's. Once again he felt
that dizzy, disoriented feeling, trapped in a strange
body that was so unlike his own.

"I'm Lars Swensen, and this is my wife, Maggie."
A plain, careworn-looking woman flashed him a
friendly smile as she handed him a mug of coffee.

Emerson hated coffee. He drank Earl Grey tea ex-
clusively. It must be the cold that made the coffee
smell so good. He took a tentative sip, and his entire
body vibrated with pleasure.

"That's it," Carrie said in a soothing voice. "Just
come into the bathroom and sit down and I'll clean up
that cut on your forehead. As soon as you have a nice
hot meal inside you, you can deal with your truck."

For some reason he wasn't in the mood to argue. If
it wasn't for the fact that he'd somehow managed to

stumble onto one of the very people he was supposed to save, he'd be out of there before anyone realized what was happening. He didn't like accepting the kindness of strangers, and it was only when he convinced himself that he had something important to gain that he gave in and followed Carrie Alexander's slender, graceful figure out of the warm, crowded kitchen.

He had another startled glimpse of himself in the bathroom mirror before she gently pushed him down onto the edge of the old claw-footed bathtub. He had plenty of opportunity to watch her as she rummaged through the medicine cabinet, pulling out hydrogen peroxide, gauze bandages, swabs and pills. She'd gotten thinner, he was sure of it. He was a firm believer in the fact that no woman could ever be too thin or too rich. Carrie certainly had a problem with the latter. Anywhere he looked carefully, he could see signs of decay. The house was falling down around her ears, a fact she seemed cheerfully oblivious to.

And she was no thinner than Margot, the dancer from the Joffrey Ballet he'd been involved with for a few months. Carrie had been a dancer, too, hadn't she? He recalled something of that sort. She certainly moved with the same sort of innate grace Margot had had. And something more. The elegance of her movements in no way conveyed the sense of self-absorption Margot's gestures had. Carrie simply seemed to be someone at ease with her slender, fluid body.

She turned back to him, and once again there was that startled expression in her blue eyes. She began dabbing peroxide on his forehead, pushing his ridiculously long hair out of the way, and she bit her lip as she concentrated.

"What's wrong?" he found himself asking, wondering again whether she knew him.

She was eye level with him, and she managed a rueful smile. "It's just that you're so beautiful."

She'd managed to startle him. "I beg your pardon?"

"Like a Renaissance sculpture. A Botticelli angel, maybe." She shook her head, laughing at herself. "You must have heard that before."

"Not recently," he said, his voice dry.

Her fingers were cool now against his flushed skin. "Well, it can't be a novel experience. You must have spent...what is it, thirty years...with that face. Surely you must be used to people's reactions by now."

"Not exactly."

She glanced at him, startled, then obviously decided to drop it. She stood up, surveying her handiwork with satisfaction. "I think you'll live," she pronounced, and it was all he could do not to snort in derision.

"I'm Carrie Alexander, by the way. And you're..."

Inspiration failed him. He reached for the first name he could think of, then shuddered when it came about. "Gabriel," he said. He thought about that strange reflection in the mirror. "Gabriel Falconi," he said, wondering why it sounded right.

Obviously she thought so, too. "It suits you. Come and meet the rest of my Thanksgiving guests. If we wait much longer my turkey will dry out." She was out of the tiny bathroom, her long skirts swirling around her ankles, and he had no choice but to follow her, protesting.

"But my truck..."

"Your truck can wait. I'm not serving cold, dried-out turkey and congealed gravy to all these people. And you look like you're in need of a good hot meal yourself. Come along. Someone will have set an extra place for you by now."

"But..."

"Come along," she repeated firmly, sounding like a cross between Augusta and Mary Poppins. She was six inches shorter than his new self, and if his age was still relevant, about four years younger, and she was acting like his mother. He didn't like it.

He was, however, interested in having his first real meal in seventeen months. If he could smell things he could probably taste them, too. And the thought of turkey and gravy, and what was almost definitely apple pie for dessert, was too much for him to resist. He didn't even have to worry about cholesterol anymore.

He was amazed that there were only eleven people at dinner. Twelve, if you counted the small scrap of humanity that slept peacefully in an old wicker basket in the corner. He'd met Lars and his wife, briefly, at least, and he was introduced to their other three children, Kirsten, with thick blond braids and an adolescent shyness, Nils, a sturdy boy in his teens, and Harald, who was just a little younger.

There were the Milsoms, a middle-aged couple who seemed clearly devoted to each other, Jeffie Baker, a sullen-looking teenager, and Gertrude Hansen, a bent-over, white-haired old lady with thick, impenetrable glasses and a sweet, gentle manner. They all welcomed him like the prodigal son, and he found himself ensconced in the middle of the huge old table, surrounded by Hansens, Swensens and their ilk. And too far away from Carrie Alexander.

Without his asking, a plate arrived in front of him, piled high with turkey, rice, gravy and biscuits. His mug of coffee had appeared by his plate, refilled, and a glass of jug wine accompanied it. He reached for his stainless steel fork, when a sudden silence fell over the chattering party.

"Would you ask the blessing, Lars?" Carrie asked, and Lars nodded.

Oh, God, he thought, writhing in embarrassment. He was going to have to sit there and listen while they prayed, for heaven's sake. He'd fallen into a bunch of religious fanatics.

Lars, however, was simple and to the point. "Bless this food which you have given to us so abundantly. Bless our friends and family, and welcome the stranger to our midst. Amen."

"Amen," the others muttered, heads bowed, and Gabriel cast a worried glance around at them. But then, the uncomfortable moment passed. People began digging into their food, and conversation was once again at fever pitch, interspersed with the occasional moment of silence as people paused to chew their food.

He kept his head down, concentrating on the meal with an almost religious fervor, hoping no one would decide to cross-examine him. Particularly when he wasn't certain what his story would be. He'd come up with a name, thank God, though it was an absurd name. He was just lucky he hadn't hit upon something worse, like Angelo. Gabriel was bad enough. A fallen angel, all right. He only wondered how much further he was going to fall before all this was through. Whether he'd be able to accomplish the overwhelming task Augusta had set before him. Or whether he'd end up in the other place.

He didn't want to go there. Bottom line, he wanted heaven, eternal happiness, wings and all that crap. At least he had a head start. Carrie Alexander was only a few feet away. He wouldn't have to hunt her down to solve whatever crisis his life had precipitated.

Though right now she didn't look very troubled. If only Augusta had been more specific. The woman sitting at the head of the table didn't look as if her life had been a series of disasters. She looked calm, happy, at peace with the world. What in the world could she want that he could possibly give her?

Three people, Augusta had said. Three people whose lives he'd destroyed. Carrie didn't look destroyed, but looks could be deceiving. And where the hell was he going to find the other two? They couldn't all be in this tiny little backwater...

He realized then that he didn't even know where he was. It might be Upstate New York or Alaska or Siberia, for all he knew. Somewhere cold and snowy. The happy din had quieted somewhat, and he drained his cup of coffee with automatic appreciation and caught Lars's eye.

"What's the name of this town?" he asked, hoping he sounded natural. He didn't dare ask what state he was in, besides the obvious state of confusion.

"Town?" Lars laughed. "I don't know if I'd call Angel Falls a town, exactly. More a dot on the map."

Gabriel's empty mug slipped out of his hand. "Angel Falls?" he echoed, getting used to the faint harshness in his new voice. This time, at least, it was justified.

"High-flown kind of name for such an unpretentious little town, isn't it?" murmured Milsom, the man next to him. "Named after the falls, of course, and they were named after the lake, and I think it was probably missionaries who named the lake some two, three hundred years ago. So we're stuck with the name, and it's gotten so most of us sort of like it."

"Especially during the Christmas season," Carrie said. She wasn't eating much, Gabriel noticed. She hadn't put much on her plate to begin with, and most of it was still there, just slightly rearranged.

"So what are you doing driving through this part of Minnesota during a snowstorm?" Lars asked. "Shouldn't you be with your family on Thanksgiving?"

"Minnesota?" he echoed, momentarily shocked.

"Where'd you think you were? Hawaii?" Jeffie Baker spoke up, breaking the sullen silence he'd maintained through most of the meal. Gabriel wished he'd continued to shut up.

"Guess I must have crossed the border without realizing it," Gabriel said.

"The border's about two hours in any direction," Lars pointed out, not unkindly. At least he let the question of family go. "What do you do for a living, Gabriel?"

"A living?" Instinctively he looked at his hands. Big hands, work worn. He hadn't the faintest idea what they were used to doing.

"Don't tell me," Lars said, and Gabriel breathed a sigh of relief. "I can tell just by looking at your hands. You're a carpenter, like me."

"Am I?" he muttered. "I mean, of course." He'd never touched a woodworking tool in his life, but at least he wouldn't be forced to prove it.

Lars held up his own hands. They were squarer, broader, but they had the same look to them. "Takes one to know one. Were you looking for work around here? Because I have to tell you, there's not much. We're a poor community since the factory closed down, and it doesn't look like things are about to improve."

"I'm not planning to take any work away from you..." Gabriel said automatically, not even wondering why he'd say such an uncharacteristic thing. Emerson would take anything he could get in his quest for success.

"You'd be welcome to it if there were any," Lars said flatly. "We've just been scraping by. There's some logging work that might be opening up before long, but I don't know if they need more than one."

"I'm not looking for work."

As if on cue, everyone looked at him, at his threadbare flannel shirt, his obvious air of less than notable prosperity. "I've got work after Christmas," he explained. "Due on the job Christmas Day, as a matter of fact. I'm just passing through, looking for a way to kill some time until the job comes up."

They seemed to swallow that. After all, it was nothing more than the truth. "Well, you're welcome to spend your time in Angel Falls. Unless you've got family...?"

There was that question again. He didn't know about Gabriel Falconi, but Emerson MacVey didn't have a relative to call his own. "No family," he said.

"We have something in common then," Carrie said, her face smooth and unlined, her voice casual. And yet he felt her pain, as sharply as he'd ever felt his own. "Orphans of the storm. Stay and spend Christmas with us, Gabriel. We're a friendly town. We share what we have, no matter how little it is."

He wished he could tell her no. He wanted to get out of this warm, friendly community, away from the concern of strangers, the gentle prying. But Carrie Alexander was one-third of his ticket to heaven.

Gertrude Hansen was seated on his other side. She put a gnarled hand on his, and her eyes behind the thick bottle-lens glasses blinked sincerely. "Stay with us, Gabriel," she said, and he was suddenly, forcibly, reminded of Augusta.

Ridiculous, of course. This stooped-over, gentle creature had nothing to do with the harridan of heaven. He tried to move his hand, but her grip was surprisingly strong. "Stay," she said again, and her sweet, soft voice was joined by a chorus of others.

"Stay," Carrie said. "You've never experienced anything until you've experienced a real Scandinavian Christmas. We're all of Norse descent around here—Swedes and Danes and Norwegians. We know how to celebrate Christmas."

"And you wouldn't believe the food," Mrs. Milsom leaned across the table to inform him.

He'd cleared the mound of food on his plate, he, who seldom ate anything more filling than nouvelle cuisine. "You've convinced me," he said, glancing toward Carrie.

It hit him, harder than the windshield of his truck, harder than the blows of the paramedics as they'd labored over his chest, harder than anything he'd felt in his short self-absorbed life. She smiled at him, her blue eyes filled with warmth and pleasure, and he was lost. The emotional pull was immediate and shocking, so intense that he felt mesmerized. It no longer mattered what his task was, what Augusta's orders were, what his observer, whoever he was, would tell him to do. It no longer mattered about the two other people he was going to save.

He had no intention of leaving Carrie Alexander's side until he was forced to do so. Come hell or high water. And he doubted high water would have anything to do with it.

Chapter Two

Carrie stood in front of the old iron sink, staring out into the windswept night as the four men trudged off into the darkness. Three men and a boy, she amended to herself, glancing at Jeffie's slight, childish frame. She was worried about him. His parents had taken off again, some joint business trip, and as far as she knew they hadn't even called to check in on him. They knew she'd have him over for Thanksgiving, and they figured their responsibility ended there.

Carrie wasn't quite sure when responsibility to your children ended, but Jeffie was only seventeen. And a very troubled seventeen-year-old at that. He needed parents, he needed people to care about him, to concern themselves with his well-being. Instead he had two workaholics who'd washed their hands of him when he'd failed to live up to their exacting standards. They still loved him, all right. They just didn't have much use for him. And Jeffie knew it.

"Let me take over," Maggie said, nudging Carrie out of the way with her comfortable bulk. "You've been on your feet all day and you look worn out. Kirsten and I can finish up these dishes."

Carrie didn't even consider making a token protest. She was exhausted, so tired she wasn't certain if she could cover it up. And she wanted to sit in a quiet place and think about the stranger who'd shown up on her doorstep.

The baby lay sleeping soundly in the old bassinet, not stirring as Carrie added more wood to the cast enamel stove. Sinking down in the shabby armchair that had once been her grandfather's favorite place in the world, she put her feet up, leaned her head back and closed her eyes.

Why did he seem so familiar? She'd never seen him before in her life, of that she was absolutely certain. If she had, she wouldn't have forgotten him. He looked like a Renaissance angel, with such classic, astonishing beauty that part of her wanted to just sit and stare at him. It had taken all her wavering concentration to keep up a normal front. She'd been working too hard, not taking proper care of herself. She knew it, and yet she couldn't change. Guilt was a powerful force in her life, one she didn't even try to combat.

Would he still be around tomorrow? He hadn't been very talkative. He said he was just passing through, and it was more than possible that once they got him out of his ditch, he'd move on, touching their lives only briefly.

But she didn't think so. She'd never been one for relying on her instincts—they'd failed her too many times. But she somehow knew that Gabriel Falconi had stumbled onto their Thanksgiving dinner for a reason. And he wasn't going to simply disappear without accomplishing whatever he'd come to do.

She shook her head, marveling at her own sudden fancifulness. She was overtired, overfed, though she'd barely eaten a thing, worn out by the stress and excitement of the day.

By the time tomorrow dawned and Gabriel Falconi drove away from Angel Falls, Minnesota, she'd see things more clearly.

A tiny snuffling sound alerted her, and she was out of the chair, lifting the sturdy bundle that was Anna Caroline Swensen into her arms. Her goddaughter, little Carrie, smiled up at her, sleepy, not yet ready to demand a feeding, and Carrie sank back down into the chair, cradling the four-month-old in her arms. "No turkey for you, little one," she murmured in a low voice. "Next Thanksgiving, maybe. If any one of us is still here."

"Is she all right?" Maggie, with the instinct of all mothers, stood in the door, her weary face momentarily lightening at the sight of her new daughter.

"She'll be demanding food before too long. I'll take your place in the kitchen..."

"I'll bring a bottle, if you wouldn't mind. She needs to get used to bottles, and to other people feeding her."

"Why?" Carrie asked flatly. "Are you having trouble nursing?"

Maggie shook her head. "I'm going to have to find work, you know that. I've waited too long already." She looked at her daughter, and her eyes filled with tears. "I'll bring the bottle."

"You aren't going to like this," Carrie whispered to the baby as her customary silent remorse swamped her. "I don't like it, either. Life isn't fair sometimes, little one. It's not fair at all."

Anna Caroline, however, wasn't so choosy. She accepted the formula with the placid good grace that she usually exhibited, and Carrie leaned back, thinking there were few experiences more peaceful than feeding a sleepy baby. So peaceful, in fact, that she didn't leap up when she heard the men return, stamping their feet on the front porch, their voices deep, jovial, that new voice, deeper, slower, joining in.

"He's not going anywhere tonight," Lars said when he poked his head in the door, his square face red and beaming, his graying blond hair wet with melted snow. "The tire's flat, the rim's bent, and I'm not too sure about the axle. Come daylight it might be better than it looks. Can you bed him down here tonight? We'd be more than happy to take him in, but we don't have space in the car..."

"Of course I will. It'll be company for Jeffie. He's not sure he likes having to stay here while his parents are out of town. Having another man around might make it more palatable."

Lars nodded. "I told him you'd insist, but he's a man who doesn't like to accept favors."

"He's not used to small towns," Carrie said, rising from the chair with silent grace, never disturbing the sleeping infant. "Let me set him straight."

Lars took his daughter in his burly arms, looking down at her with complete devotion. "You do that, Carrie," he murmured absently. "I've never known a man who didn't toe the line when you told him to."

"Flatterer," Carrie said dryly, walking into the kitchen.

Gabriel was standing by the sink, drying the dishes. He glanced at her when she walked in, then immediately began polishing the old Meissen that had been passed down from her great-grandmother. Once again she was struck by the palpable intensity his presence brought into the room. And the odd, impossible feeling that she knew him from somewhere.

"You're stuck with Jeffie and me for the night," she announced cheerfully. "Don't bother arguing. You can't sleep in your truck, you'll freeze to death."

"A motel..." he suggested, not looking at her.

She wanted to see his eyes again. "Not for forty miles. No hotel, no boardinghouse, and the bed-and-breakfast places up by the lake are closed for the winter. You're stuck here, Gabriel."

"I don't like to be beholden to anyone." It was odd, the way the words seemed to surprise him when they came from his mouth.

"Don't worry, you won't be. I have a nice big wood box that needs filling, more firewood outside that could use some stacking. I've got things that need doing if you've got the desire to do them."

"I've got the desire," he said, and she got her wish. He looked at her, his eyes dark, almost black, in his face, and she felt herself slipping, falling, lost in a place that was foreign and yet familiar.

She stepped back, reaching behind her for the doorway, and she smiled briskly, remembering Lars's words. She could make any man toe the line, could she? She might run into a little trouble with this one if she didn't make certain things clear right away. Like the fact that she was no-nonsense, maternal, and a friend to all. Not a potential bedmate.

"Terrific," she said briskly. "We'll put you on the sofa, and first thing in the morning we'll get Steve and his tow truck out here. Assuming Steve's back from his mother's. We'll get you up and running again, and then you can decide whether you want to stay around here until your next job comes up."

He was still watching her, and she wished she'd never noticed his eyes in the first place. Now she couldn't look away. She couldn't rid herself of the notion that she'd looked into those eyes before. Except that they'd been a different color, held a different expression.

"Absurd," she muttered beneath her breath. Was she going to have to add delusions to her list of future symptoms?

He set the dish down on the pile, folding the faded linen dish towel in his big, strong hands. "I thought I'd stay," he said. "That is, if I can find a place closer than forty miles away."

Carrie glanced at Lars and Maggie, remembering their huge old house, made for a family of twelve, and their dwindling cash supply. "I have an idea or two," she murmured. "In the meantime, who wants to play charades?"

Gabriel blinked, just a momentary reaction, and she noticed his eyelashes were absurdly long. Typical, she thought, searching for her sense of humor. Just as she had decided to ignore her own selfish wants and embark on a mission to right the wrongs she'd inadvertently done, someone had sent her the most potent package of temptation she'd seen in her entire life.

Lars went over and slung an arm around Gabriel's shoulders. "Come along, Gabe," he boomed. "We'll show them a thing or two."

"Yeah," Jeffie piped up, for the first time not sullen. "Men against the women. We'll beat the stuffing out of them." And he looked up at Gabriel with shy, burgeoning adoration.

Lord, I hope I don't look the same, Carrie thought. "Wanna bet? Loser does the dishes tomorrow morning."

"Aw, Carrie..."

"Aw, Carrie, nothing," she said. "Don't you have any faith in your ability to stomp on us poor defenseless women?"

Jeffie cast another glance at Gabriel's unpromising expression. "We've got an unknown quantity on our side," he pointed out.

"Maybe I shouldn't play," Gabriel said in his slow, deep voice.

"Nonsense. What better way can we get to know someone? Especially since he's going to be around till Christmas. It's a trial by fire," Lars boomed.

"Trial by fire," Gabriel echoed. "That sounds about right." But the fire was in the depth of his dark, dangerous eyes. And despite the warmth of the old kitchen, Carrie shivered.

HE WAS ABOUT A FOOT too long for the sofa. Tucking his arms under his head, Gabriel stared up at the ceiling, watching the faint shimmers of light that filtered from the minuscule cracks in the wood stove. Emerson would have fit on the sofa, he thought. But not Gabriel. His feet hung over the end, his size-thirteen feet, he'd discovered when he'd taken off his snow-wet sneakers. His backbone was curved against the lumpy cushions, and his head was throbbing. He was probably going to be a mass of stiffened muscles when he woke up the next morning. But at least he'd be warm enough. The wood stove was kicking out the heat, and the quilt that covered him was thick, beautiful and smothering. If he could just manage to clear his mind of all the distractions he would manage to sleep.

Problem was, he didn't want to. Never had life seemed so precious to him, now, in the quiet of the fire lit living room of the old farmhouse. He could hear the wind howling outside, the dry crackle of the firewood, the solid chunk as a piece broke apart in the flames. He could hear Jeffie snoring faintly, in a bedroom miles away at the rear of the house. He could hear Carrie breathing in the room above him, hear the faint, steady beat of her heart. He could even hear the flakes of snow as they dropped to the ground.

He felt odd, disoriented, thrust into a life that was as foreign to him as if he'd landed on Mars. Even the things that should have been familiar seemed somehow different. The taste of turkey, for instance. A hundred times better than he'd ever remembered. And coffee. Strong, biting, absolutely delicious.

Lars's hearty friendship, Bill Milsom's shyer warmth, were things that were foreign, as well. As was Jeffie Baker, for some obscure reason staring up at him as if he were God walking the earth instead of an itinerant carpenter who'd managed to land himself in a ditch on a snowy night.

This would be a dangerous place to live, he thought. You might start believing in people, in things. And then where would you be?

He closed his eyes, shifting uncomfortably on the couch, and he knew it wasn't the lumpy cushion that was making him restless. It was that damned game of charades.

He hadn't played charades since he was ten years old and at summer camp. Even then he'd thought it was an impossibly stupid game, juvenile and idiotic. He never would have thought adults would play it, and enjoy it. He never thought he'd be shouting out answers, completely involved. Until it had been Carrie Alexander's turn.

He'd vaguely known she was a dancer, but it hadn't meant anything to him. Until she'd risen and walked to the center of the room, elegant, simple grace radiating from her reed-slim body. He didn't even know what she'd been trying to act out. He hadn't heard the shouts from the women as they tried to guess, hadn't been aware of anything but the twist and flow of her, slow and sensuous and supple.

Hunger hadn't been his only physical appetite to return, he realized with a shock. Staring at Carrie Alexander, he knew a longing that was both intensely sexual and far beyond that. He wanted her with a need he'd never felt before. A need that shook him to the very marrow of his bones. A need he had no intention of giving in to. If he did, it would be an express ticket to hell.

But lying alone in that living room, he could give in to the fantasy. He could look through the darkness and imagine she was there again, moving, twisting, dancing, just for him. And then he shut his eyes tight, closing off the half-remembered vision, and let out a quiet, agonized groan. If he didn't make it through this sojourn, hell might end up being a picnic.

Another noise suddenly overwhelmed the intense peacefulness of the old house. A faint scrabbling sound that at first he identified as the never-before-heard sound of mice in the woodwork. And then he heard another sound, or lack thereof. Jeffie had stopped snoring.

He kept his breathing steady, not moving, as he listened to the sound of a door creak open. Someone was moving in the kitchen, someone so still and silent that Gabriel felt his heart stop. For a crazed, longing moment he thought it might be Carrie, coming to him. A moment later he dismissed the thought as patently absurd. Then he saw Jeffie's shadow on the wall in the kitchen as he reached across the table. For the half-empty bottle of wine.

None of his business, Gabriel told himself. The boy was close enough to drinking age, and it wasn't his problem. He wasn't here to save Jeffie Baker.

"You think you ought to be doing that?" He could hardly believe the quiet voice was coming from the stranger's body he was currently inhabiting. "After all, she's a good lady, welcoming you into her home, feeding you, making you welcome. Is that any way to repay her?" He pitched his voice so low it would carry no farther than the kitchen. He kept the reproach out of it—simply giving Jeffie the choice.

The shadow was absolutely motionless. And then the bottle was replaced, untouched, on the table, and the phantom figure moved away. A moment later he heard the sound of the door closing once more.

"Damn," he muttered beneath his breath. He should have kept his mouth shut. Who was he to give advice, opinions, admonishments? Who was he to involve himself in other people's problems, when his own were beyond overwhelming, beyond life threatening? They were eternal.

He had no idea whether he'd made Jeffie's situation better or worse. He told himself he didn't care, but the odd thing was, he did. For no reason at all, it mattered to him. He didn't want to see an already troubled boy get mired even deeper into the kind of mess life could be.

It wasn't until he heard the faint, measured sound of Jeffie's snoring that he let some of the tension drain out of his body. He hadn't even realized he'd been wired, until he let go of it. At least he hadn't traumatized the boy. Maybe he just needed someone to point out a few things to him. It wasn't his job, it was his parents'. Clearly they hadn't been meeting their responsibilities.

And then his body froze again as he heard the almost imperceptible sounds of someone moving through the old house. Not Jeffie this time—he was still snoring lightly. That left only one person, moving down the narrow, steep stairs, coming toward him, dressed in a filmy negligee, reaching out for him ...

She wasn't wearing a filmy negligee, she was wearing an enveloping flannel nightgown that reached almost down to her narrow toes. Her straight blond hair was tousled with sleep, her face open and vulnerable as she moved into the living room, silent as a wraith.

And he knew she hadn't come for a romp on the narrow sofa with a horny stranger.

She sat down on the rocking chair opposite him. She was wearing a shawl over the white nightgown, and as she pulled it closer around her chilled body he considered asking her if she wanted to share the quilt. He didn't. He just sat up on the sofa, waiting.

"Thank you," she said, her musical voice pitched so low he could just hear it.

"For what?"

"For Jeffie. It was so stupid of me, to leave the wine out. I was too tired to think straight."

"You knew there was a problem?"

"I know Jeffie has a lot of problems. I can't lock everything away and keep him from himself. But I don't have to waft temptation under his nose."

He looked at her, and knew a lot about temptation wafting under his nose. "He's not my responsibility."

"Of course not. Any more than he's mine. But that doesn't keep me from doing whatever good I can along the way."

"What will it get you in the end?" he countered, playing the devil's advocate. He'd spent his entire life looking out for himself, and himself alone.

She shrugged her narrow shoulders beneath the thick shawl, a self-deprecating smile on her face. "A place in heaven?" she suggested.

He shut his eyes for a moment, wishing he even had the faith to say, why me, Lord? But he didn't. He'd had too much of coincidences, of not-so-subtle reminders, of Angel Falls, Minnesota, and the vulnerable-looking woman opposite him whom he couldn't remember wanting when he could have had her. Now that she was out of reach he seemed to have developed an instantaneous obsession.

"I'm not going to worry about that," he said finally. "I expect I'm a lost cause."

"No one's a lost cause. You helped Jeffie tonight, even if your brain told you not to bother. I think you've got good instincts."

"I don't believe in instincts. I believe in facts." That was Emerson talking, Gabriel realized. His old pragmatic self.

"If you say so," Carrie said, rising from the rocking chair and opening the wood stove. She reached into the wood box for a thick log, and he was up off the sofa before he realized what he was doing, taking the wood out of her hand.

For a moment she didn't move, didn't release her grip on the heavy log. She was shorter than he remembered, coming up to his chin. But no, he was taller than he remembered, that was it. He wasn't wearing a shirt, and his jeans were zipped but unsnapped, and if she made the mistake of looking downward she'd find he was far from immune to her presence, to the enveloping flannel nightgown, to the faint, flowery scent of her.

She didn't look down. She looked up into his eyes, but the startled awareness was there all the same. Identical to the sudden, sure knowledge that rippled through his body, and he wanted to toss the log across the room and take her slender body into his arms.

He didn't, of course. Enough of the old Emerson remained to keep him reasonably well behaved. She released the piece of wood and stepped back, letting him load the stove with more force than dexterity.

When he'd closed the door he found she was out of reach, standing by the kitchen.

"Thanks again," she said, her voice smooth and warm, devoid of any kind of sexual awareness.

Maybe he'd imagined that heated moment. But he didn't think so. She was aware of him, as he was of her. But she'd pulled her defenses around her as tightly as that shawl, presenting a friendly, sisterly front.

He wanted to cross the room in two quick strides, pull the shawl away from her and explain to her in definite physical terms that he had no need of a sister. He didn't move.

"Anytime," he murmured.

She disappeared then as silently as a ghost, and he heard her light footsteps as they moved quickly up the stairs again. The wood stove was radiating heat, but he barely noticed it. He was so damned hot already.

First thing tomorrow morning he needed to get his truck out of the ditch, get the tire repaired and get the hell away from temptation. There was no way he could save her if he slept with her. She didn't need a lover who was going to disappear on Christmas Eve. She needed commitment, a man to cherish her, till death do them part. He'd already passed that point.

He was half tempted to get away from Angel Falls altogether. He had no more faith than the imperial Augusta had in his ability to accomplish his mission. Maybe he ought to give up before he started, enjoy his month and take his punishment like a man.

He didn't even know what Carrie needed from him. Where her life needed fixing, what damage he'd caused her. She looked happy enough. She had friends, a charming if slightly tumbledown house. What was missing? What was broken?

But eternity was too high a stake to wager. And he couldn't remember anything in life that would be worth giving up a chance at heaven. He was going to tough it out, he was going to win, damn it. He wasn't a man who admitted defeat. He had a month, he had three miracles, and he'd already found one of the people he had to save. If he could just keep his raging hormones under control he'd do fine.

He sank back down onto the uncomfortable sofa, thinking about the woman sleeping overhead. Except she wasn't sleeping. She was lying upstairs, her eyes open, staring at the ceiling, just as he was. And sleep was going to be impossible tonight.

For both of them.

Chapter Three

Carrie lay alone in the big bed, the bed she'd never shared, and waited for sleep to come. The snow had finally stopped—moonlight was streaming through the frosted-up window, sending shadow patterns across the old, faded rug.

Odd, Carrie thought, shifting around, looking for a comfortable spot on the wide mattress. She'd never thought about the bed being lonely before. But she was thinking about it tonight. And thinking about the man downstairs. Hovering over her, so damned big and yet not the slightest bit threatening.

At least, not in the usual sense. Gabriel Falconi was a threat. To her peace of mind. To her carefully acquired plan of celibacy and self-sacrifice. To the safe little cocoon she'd spun around her.

It would be easier if he wasn't so extraordinarily beautiful. It would be easier if he wasn't so troubled, so obviously torn by conflict. She wanted to soothe him, comfort him, help him. She already owed so much to so many people. She could just add him to her list. She could do her best to help Jeffie, the Swensens, Gertrude and the Milsoms, she could save

Gabriel, and she could deny herself and her own self-ish wants.

An odd thought. Why should Gabriel need saving? He was clearly better off than Lars Swensen—at least he had a job to go to in another month. He didn't have six hungry mouths to feed, a mortgage to meet, a crushing sense of failure that was in no way his due.

But Gabriel had something eating at him. Darkness lurked behind his eyes, a darkness of the soul. And Carrie had the uneasy suspicion that his demons might prove too much even for her.

Her room was cold. She usually left the doors open to let the heat circulate, but tonight she wanted to be closed in, with barriers of wood between her and the man stretched out on her grandmother's old couch. She couldn't save everyone, fix everything. It was her foolish need to do so that had gotten Angel Falls into the disaster it was in. And Carrie had every intention of paying her debts. Not amassing new ones.

WHEN SHE AWOKE sunlight was streaming in the old multipaned windows, spreading across the quilt that covered her, reaching to her fingertips. She lay without moving, absorbing the heat, slowly coming to wakefulness. She had a reason to wake up today, something exciting had happened, but in the first mists of sleep she couldn't remember what.

She glanced over at the old windup alarm clock. It must have stopped last night, and she'd never noticed. It said ten-thirty, and she never slept past six in the morning nowadays.

But she could hear the steady ticking, a loud, comforting noise. She could hear another, rhythmic thud, coming from outside. And she remembered why she was happy. Too late to keep from feeling that pleasure. Gabriel was here.

Snow was melting from the trees outside her bedroom window as she quickly threw on some clothes. The storm last night was leaving as quickly as it had come, the thick wet snow disappearing. She frowned for a moment, leaning her head against the pane of glass. She'd been ready for snow. Once Thanksgiving came, it was part of the whole Christmas season, a welcome enough part as long as it didn't choose to storm on a day she planned to go shopping.

She wouldn't be doing much shopping this year, nor would most of Angel Falls, with the factory shut down. It was going to be a homemade Christmas, and probably better for it.

She could smell coffee, and she hoped it was Gabriel, not Jeffie, who'd made it. Jeffie had brewed it a couple of days before, and it had taken all her limited acting ability to choke down two cups of the stuff, which was closer to toxic waste than French roast.

There was no sign of either visitor when she reached the kitchen. She poured herself a cup of coffee, noticing with relief that the color was a normal dark brown, not black sludge. There were clean dishes in the drainer, and the heat in the room came from a freshly stoked wood stove, as well as the bright sunlight. She moved toward the row of windows, mug of coffee in her hand, and looked out.

They'd been busy, the two of them. There was a pile of freshly split wood in the melting snow. Jeffie was nowhere in sight. But Gabriel was there, in the warm winter sun. Stripped to the waist, he was splitting the oversize firewood.

She couldn't move. She was mesmerized by the ripple and play of the muscles in his strong back. By the faint sheen of sweat on his golden skin. He'd tied his hair back with a discarded strip of quilting material, out of the way, and his long, muscled arms moved in a steady, hypnotic rhythm.

She'd deliberately kept herself from thinking about his body when she'd gone back up to bed last night. His face was troublesome enough, his almost angelic beauty that still managed to be completely masculine. When he'd come so close to her the night before, she'd been mesmerized. By the smooth golden texture of his skin. The corded sinew of muscle and bone beneath that skin. The faint tracery of dark hair, not too much, not too little. The long, long legs, the narrow hips. Everything about him entranced her, brought back feelings she thought she'd managed to squash down permanently. They were back in full force as she stood in the window of her old kitchen and watched a stranger work on her woodpile.

He must have felt her eyes on him. He turned suddenly, looking back at the house, and through the old window his eyes met hers. And she realized with sudden faintness that his beautiful face, his strong, sexy body, were nothing, nothing at all, compared to the siren lure of his dark, troubled eyes.

And then the spell was broken as Steve's tow truck lumbered up her winding driveway, dragging a rusty old pickup truck. Jeffie was riding in the front seat, next to Steve, and he looked like a normal, excited seventeen-year-old. If only he always looked like that.

"She's all messed up," Jeffie called out jovially as he bounced out of the truck.

Gabriel turned to look at his vehicle, and his expression was pardonably dismayed. Dropping the maul, he reached for his abandoned flannel shirt and started toward the tow truck. The conversation was too low-pitched for Carrie to hear, and she stilled her curiosity. She could see well enough that his truck wasn't going to take him away from Angel Falls for the next few days at least. That was enough for now.

Draining her now-lukewarm coffee, she headed for the telephone. It didn't take her long to accomplish her objectives, so that by the time Jeffie and Gabriel walked into the kitchen, accompanied, of course, by Steve, she had everything neatly arranged.

"His truck's real messed up, Carrie," Steve, a balding, cheerful bachelor in his late forties, announced as he took her automatically proffered cup of coffee. "I'm gonna have to order a new wheel, and that axle'll be a bitch to straighten. I told Gabe here that he's gonna have to get used to spending a few days at the back of beyond."

Carrie glanced over at Gabriel, who shrugged. "That's easy enough to say in a place that doesn't have a motel."

"I've taken care of that," Carrie announced cheerfully.

"Have you, now?" There was no reprimand in his low, even tone, but nevertheless Carrie felt some of her buoyancy vanish. She was used to taking care of people—in a small town like Angel Falls everyone looked out for one another, and she made it her business to make sure everyone was taken care of. She'd forgotten what it was like out in the real world. Where everyone had his or her own space and didn't like other people invading it. Where no one wanted to accept favors or let other people do for them. Out in the real world people wanted to control their own destinies, and most of them spent fruitless years trying to do just that.

"I've done it again, haven't I?" she asked, her voice rueful. "I was just trying to be helpful, and I got carried away. I'm sorry. I haven't committed you to anything. I just checked with Lars and Maggie to make sure they had room for you, if you wanted to board with them. You need a place, they could do with a little extra cash."

He didn't say a word, letting her babble. Once again she got the strange sense of dichotomy, almost a schizophrenia. On the one hand, he clearly wanted to tell her to stuff her concern. On the other hand, he seemed to be leaning toward accepting her help.

"Anyway," she continued, "it's a place you can stay if you need to. And if you don't have any money I know they'd be more than happy to put you up anyway. I just thought it would be a way to solve both your problems."

"Is that what you do, Carrie? Solve people's problems?" There was no edge to the question he asked. It was simply put, curious. And yet she felt oddly guilty.

"Course, it is," Steve said jovially, oblivious to the undercurrents in the room. "We count on Carrie around here. Course, she can't work miracles. She can't stop the factory from closing, she can't raise the dead. But she comes darn close."

There was an odd expression in Gabriel's dark eyes. "Darn close," he echoed softly. "As a matter of fact, I've got some money. Not a lot, but I have to live somewhere until my next job, and Angel Falls seems as good a place as any. If the Swensens will take me I'll be glad to stay there."

She felt slightly encouraged. "I might be able to come up with a little work for you. There's not much in town right now, what with the factory shutting down, but this house could do with a little shoring up before winter really hits."

To her relief he didn't get that cold, distant expression again. "Before winter hits? What was last night?"

Steve laughed. "Last night was just a lick and a promise. When the snows really come you'll know it. Matter of fact, if you're staying, either here or anywhere north of Kansas, you're gonna be needing some snow tires on that truck of yours."

"I don't know if my finances will go that far."

"Maybe we can work something out. You could give me a hand at the garage to pay off your bill. Even in a depression people still need to keep their cars running."

"I don't know anything about cars."

Steve looked startled. "That's funny. You seemed to have a pretty good sense of what you were doing when I opened the hood out there."

"If Gabriel says he doesn't know anything about cars then he doesn't," Jeffie piped up, instantly defensive. "Do you think he's lying to you?"

"Calm down, kid," Steve said. "I wasn't meaning no offense. I just thought it was odd, is all."

"Well, you can..."

"Never mind," Gabriel overrode Jeffie's protest. "I've got good instincts, but not much knowledge. Let's see how the current bill goes and we'll take it from there."

"Sure thing," Steve said. "I'll just tow her into town now. Want a ride? I'll be going right past the Swensens."

"Carrie can drive him," Jeffie announced.

"Who says she wants to?" Steve was getting a little testy at this point, and Carrie decided it was time to intervene. She was beginning to feel a little like a juicy bone, being fought over by two hungry dogs. She knew perfectly well that Steve harbored certain fruitless romantic feelings toward her. What was new was Jeffie's possessiveness. She didn't have any illusions that he might have suddenly developed an adolescent crush on her. He wanted her for Gabriel.

As for the stranger, he hadn't said a word. If he knew what was going on, he gave no sign of it. His eyes met hers, and she felt that icy-warm shiver reach down to her toes. "If you're willing to wait, I'll drive you in a couple of hours," she said. "Jeffie needs to get some fresh clothes, and I wanted to get a start on my Christmas shopping."

She startled him into breaking the mesmerizing eye contact. "Christmas shopping?" he echoed, obviously aghast. "Today?"

"It's tradition," Steve explained. "People always go Christmas shopping the day after Thanksgiving."

"That's why it's the most crowded day of the year," Gabriel protested.

"That's what's so much fun about it," Carrie said. "I usually don't even buy anything. I just like the crowds and excitement."

"You're crazy," he said flatly.

"A little."

Jeffie was looking worried. For some reason he seemed to have decided that Gabriel was the best thing since sliced bread, despite or perhaps because of their little run-in last night. While his newfound hero worship was extreme, Jeffie was still fairly protective of her. He clearly didn't like the idea of sparks between the two of them. But he wasn't sure which side to be on.

"As long as you don't drag me shopping," Gabriel said.

"I don't think anybody could drag you anywhere you didn't want to go."

"I hope you're right," he said obscurely. "Jeffie and I will fill the wood boxes. After that, you can show me what you want done around here."

That easily he'd turned things around, taking control. Suddenly she was on the receiving end, and she wasn't sure she liked it. She accepted it, however, with good grace. She nodded, turning to Steve, who'd been watching all this with a preoccupied expression on his face. "Would you like any more coffee?"

He roused himself with an effort. "Nah, I've got to get going. I want to finish in time to do a little shopping myself. I have to get something for my best girl." He gave her a meaningful leer, one she responded to with a faint smile, and then Steve followed Jeffie out into the cool morning air.

Gabriel was still standing there, an odd expression on his face. "Best girl?" he echoed.

She wanted to tell him it wasn't any of his business, as it certainly wasn't. She wanted to go into lengthy explanations, all of which would have told too much and not enough. She countered with a question of her own. "What's it to you?"

"Nothing. Nothing at all." He started toward the door, his back rigid, and she made the major mistake of not dropping it there.

"He's a friend," she said. "I have lots of friends."

He stopped at the door, not turning around. "He wants more," he said.

"I know. I don't give more. To anyone." She said it, out loud, clear and simple.

He turned to look at her then, a disturbed expression in his dark eyes, and she wondered if he was simply surprised by her statement. Or disbelieving. He'd felt the pull between the two of them as strongly as she had. She knew it.

But he didn't argue. He simply nodded, accepting. Agreeing. And then followed Jeffie out into the bright winter sunlight.

HE'D NEVER SPLIT firewood before in his life. He'd been grateful that Carrie had slept late, no witness to his miserable early attempts at turning a solid chunk of log into firewood.

Jeffie had tried to show him, but he was at that gangly, postadolescent age, all arms and legs and gawky gracelessness. Besides, he'd been so eager to please that his clumsiness had increased, so that even Gabriel's feeble attempts had shown better results.

He hadn't said anything about the late-night visit to
the kitchen. Indeed, Jeffie had studiously avoided
mentioning it, being careful to fill any possible con-
versational openings with lively, slightly nervous
chatter that precluded anything more meaningful.
Gabriel was glad to leave it at that. He still didn't quite
understand why he'd interfered the night before, and
he wasn't eager to get even more involved. For some
reason Jeffie, instead of resenting his interference,
seemed almost pathetically grateful.

Gabriel took the wood-splitting instruction with
good grace, discovering, if he just forgot to think
about it, his body took over, falling into the rhythm
with a naturalness that made his previous claims of
knowing nothing about wood seem a blatant lie.

The same had happened with the pickup. When
Steve had finally managed to drag the poor old wreck
up the road, Gabriel had opened the hood with unerring instinct, poked around at parts he couldn't
name, his hands knowing what his brain didn't.

He'd have to watch himself. At this rate, Jeffie
would start thinking he was an alien. *Invasion of the
Body Snatchers* wasn't far-off.

He couldn't help but wonder if there really was a
Gabriel Falconi somewhere. A tall, muscular Italian
carpenter with the face of a Botticelli angel. If so, what
happened to him? Had he died, too? Or was he simply a figment of Augusta's sourly twisted imagination?

It didn't really matter. What mattered was getting
through the next month in one piece. He was supposed to save three people. One of whom he'd already
discovered. She was obviously his first priority—he'd

have to assume someone would lead him in the direction of the other two once he'd taken care of Carrie.

He didn't want to be led away from her. He didn't want to save her. When he let his imagination drift, he found he really wanted to debauch her in some pleasant, mutually agreeable manner. She'd warned him off with words, with body language. But her eyes said something completely different.

What the hell was wrong with her? How was he going to save her, when he'd made such a mess of his own life? And how was he going to be around her for however long it took without touching her? Kissing her? Pushing her down onto that lumpy sofa that had been more torture rack than bed and making love to her on that beautiful quilt?

"You got any kids, Gabriel?" Jeffie asked as he arranged the firewood in an artistic configuration.

"No. But I'm only thirty-two years old."

"I've got a brother who's thirty-two."

Gabriel stopped what he was doing, looking over at the boy with the deliberately casual stance and the wary expression in his eyes.

"Do you? Does he live around here?"

Jeffie shrugged. "No one really knows where he is. He dropped out of college, joined some commune years ago. Every now and then he sends my parents some book about enlightenment."

"What does he send you?"

Jeffie's smile was twisted. "I think he's forgotten about me. I was only five when he left. I think he's up in Alaska now. Becoming one with the seals, or something like that."

"Sounds pretty flaky."

"That's what my parents say. They're pretty disappointed in him. Guess that's what parenting's all about. Disappointment."

Gabriel had a tendency to agree, but different words came out. "I don't know about that. I think being a parent's probably the most important thing anyone can do."

"Not if you ask my parents." Jeffie dropped another log onto the pile, and the neat stack collapsed in a welter of firewood. He swore at them, something quite astonishingly obscene, and Gabriel, who used such words frequently, had to hite hack an uncharacteristic reproof. Jeffie would have to learn by himself not to use those words indiscriminately. Gabriel wasn't going to lecture him.

Besides, Jeffie wasn't his particular problem. Carrie was. "What do you think about her?" he asked casually.

Jeffie looked confused for a moment. "You mean Carrie? She's pretty neat, considering. I mean, she's like all grown-ups. Wants to take care of you, when you're old enough to take care of yourself."

"I noticed," Gabriel said dryly, thinking of her heavy-handed attempts to get him safely settled in Angel Falls.

"But she's still pretty cool. She'll do anything for anybody, no matter what it costs her, she's always willing to help out, and besides, she's the best cook I know. She never lectures, and she'll give me a ride anytime I call her, no questions asked. Like I said, she's neat."

It was a lot of information crammed into one artless speech. Gabriel picked it apart carefully, going for the most important aspect. "What do you mean, she'll do anything for anybody, no matter what it costs her?"

A variety of expressions crossed Jeffie's face. Remorse, furtiveness, guilt. "I'm not supposed to talk about it."

"Too late, you already did," Gabriel snapped, not caring if he sounded cold. He was going to get it out of Jeffie if he had to beat it out of him.

"Listen, I promised . . ."

Gabriel set the maul down and advanced on Jeffie. "You're about to break your promise. What did you mean?"

He heard the door open behind him as Carrie left the house. She was still out of earshot, but he only had a moment.

"Tell me," he said, "or I'll ask her."

"Don't do that, man," Jeffie said wildly.

"Tell me."

Jeffie glanced behind him at Carrie's approaching figure. "She doesn't take care of herself," he finally admitted. "She got pneumonia and almost died last year, she's accident-prone, and no one can get her to slow down. Maggie says she just doesn't care about herself anymore. She's punishing herself, and no one knows why. Maggie says something happened to her in New York, something that changed her, and sooner or later she's going to walk in front of a truck or something again, and there's not a damned thing anyone can do about it." He stopped, breathless, defiant, glaring at his newfound hero. "She's going to die, damn it. Unless someone can find a way to save her. And I don't believe in miracles."

Gabriel looked across the snow-covered ground as she approached. "Neither do I," he said in a low voice. "But we both might be surprised."

Chapter Four

Carrie Alexander drove an aging Japanese station wagon that had seen better days, but not, in Emerson Wyatt MacVey III's opinion, much better. Its muffler was making a loud, throaty rumble, the bumper was held on by a wire, the once-maroon paint was liberally splattered with rust, and the windshield was cracked. He climbed into the front seat, trying to stretch his too-long legs out in front of him, and stared at the pitted vinyl dashboard, the mileage counter that read well above one hundred thousand miles. It did, however, start on the first try.

"Good baby," Carrie crooned, reaching out a slender hand and stroking the aging dashboard as a mother strokes a child.

"You talk to your cars?" he asked, mesmerized by her hand, the long, delicate fingers, the unconscious sensuality of her caress. And the waste of it, on an inanimate old car that belonged in a junkyard.

She glanced over at him, and there was a glint of humor in her bright blue eyes. "Everything on this earth needs a little encouragement now and then. I've learned not to take anything for granted, including having a car start when it's supposed to."

"I don't wonder, with this car," he said wryly.

"It's not in that much worse shape than your truck."

"My truck's been in an accident."

"You know what I mean. Besides, it's a waste of time bemoaning the fact that you don't have a Mercedes when you'll never afford one. It's better to be happy with what you have."

He had owned a Mercedes, a car he'd taken for granted. He'd certainly never stroked the dashboard and crooned lovingly to the motor. "This is a very nice car," he said.

"It's going to get you into town, which is a lot better than walking," she replied cheerfully, putting the car into reverse and backing out the long, curving driveway without looking.

He didn't look, either, too busy watching her face and thinking about Jeffie's disclosures. It had to have been typical teenage dramatics, but Carrie had come up on them too quickly for Gabriel to cross-examine him. He'd have to wait till he had a few moments alone with Jeffie to beat it out of him, if need be.

What had happened to her in New York that had changed her? It wasn't MacVey—he refused to accept responsibility. But then, if he wasn't responsible, why was he here now? He had miracles, Augusta had told him. Perhaps he could simply mutter a few hookie-pookie words and Carrie would start taking better care of herself. First task accomplished, and then he could be on his way.

He didn't think it was going to be that simple. Even if he'd been given some miraculous healing touch, where all he had to do was reach out to the woman by his side and solve her problems, it wouldn't solve his. He wasn't ready to move on. Away from here. He wasn't ready to go anywhere. Even to heaven and some kind of eternal bliss.

"Do you want me to drop you off at your house, Jeffie, or do you want to come with us to Swensens'?" she asked, navigating the slush-covered roads with a singular lack of attention. The four-wheel drive vehicle held the road surprisingly well despite its decrepit appearance, and Gabriel forced himself to relax in the front seat. He'd never enjoyed being driven—he was a man who liked to be in control of his own destiny at all times. He'd had to accept the fact that never again would he control anything in his life.

"I'll come with you," Jeffie said promptly from the back seat. "Maybe Lars will let me work in the shop for a while."

"Are you making something for your parents?" Gabriel asked.

Jeffie snorted. "Not likely. I just like messing around with wood."

"So do I," Gabriel said without thinking, then stopped, surprised. He glanced down at his hands again, those large work-worn hands, and wondered what talents lay beneath the skin and bone and sinew.

"I have to stop by the drugstore on the way," Carrie said as they pulled into a small town. "Henry's closing early to go Christmas shopping. Do either of you need anything?"

"Are you sick?" Gabriel asked abruptly, remembering the pneumonia that had nearly killed her.

"Oh, man," Jeffie muttered in the back seat.

Carrie's cheerful expression didn't waver. "Nothing that a little aspirin won't cure," she said, parking outside a small storefront with the gilt-lettered Olsen's Pharmacy peeling off the windows. There was a Christmas tree in the window, a fake silver one, and the lights were flashing off and on with dizzying regularity.

"I'm coming with you," Jeffie said, reaching for the door.

Gabriel put his hand out and stopped him. "No, you're not," he said pleasantly. "Keep me company and tell me about this town."

Telling about a town the size of Angel Falls would take exactly thirty seconds, but Jeffie settled back, a mutinous expression on his face as he muttered again, "Oh, man."

Gabriel waited until Carrie disappeared inside the store. "So?"

"So what?" Jeffie responded.

"She's not going to be in there that long, and if you don't tell me now I'll ask you when she gets back out here. What did you mean, she's changed? That she's going to walk in front of another truck or something. Are you telling me she's suicidal?"

"Not exactly. She just doesn't look after herself, and around here life is tough enough that you need to. She's so busy taking care of everyone else that she forgets to eat, doesn't watch where she's going. Maggie says if she doesn't pull herself together it's only a matter of time before something terrible happens."

Gabriel digested all that unwillingly. "How has she changed since she was in New York?"

Jeffie shrugged. "I don't know, man. Neither does anyone else. Maybe she's just still run-down from the accident."

"What accident?"

"Man," said Jeffie, shaking his head, "that's where it all started. She walked in front of a taxi in New York City and nearly got killed. Apparently it was Christmas Eve, she'd just been fired from her job, and she was so upset she didn't watch where she was going." Jeffie stared out at the busy sidewalk. "I'd like to get my hands on the bastard who fired her."

"Who says it was his fault?" Gabriel said, trying not to squirm. "He didn't push her in front of the cab, did he?"

"Carrie still defends the pig. All I know is she nearly died. When she got back here, she was different. Quieter, sadder than anyone remembered. Whatever money she has goes to everyone else, and I know for a fact she barely has enough to get by on."

"Maybe she ought to put that energy into herself," Gabriel argued. "She needs to get a job, feed herself..."

"There aren't any jobs around here. She can't make enough quilts to support the entire town, and Maggie says that's what she's trying to do."

"Is that what she does? Makes quilts?"

"Man, don't you notice anything?" Jeffie's hero worship was fading fast, something that ought to have relieved Gabriel. Instead, he felt curiously bereft.

He tried to stretch his legs out in front of him. "Sometimes I'm extremely unobservant," he said with a weary sigh.

"Hey, I'm sorry, I forgot you hit your head," Jeffie said, suddenly contrite. "You must be feeling like garbage, and here I'm bothering you with Carrie's problems."

"You're not bothering me," Gabriel said flatly. "I want to know how I can help her."

"You and everybody else. There's nothing we can do. Unless you happen to have a miracle available. Fat chance," Jeffie said with all the true cynicism of a seventeen-year-old.

"You'd be surprised," Gabriel said mildly, watching as Carrie left the store and moved toward the car with her usual grace.

She didn't look as if she were an accident waiting to happen. She was too thin and pale, but her eyes were bright, her soft mouth was smiling, and he wondered what had happened to her to make her feel that life wasn't worth living. He couldn't remember anything about the three months she'd been one of his secretaries—most of his past was a frustrating blank. But he hadn't been a monster; surely he couldn't have destroyed her life.

He wanted to take her narrow shoulders and shake some sense into her. Right now life seemed very precious indeed to him, and he couldn't stand the thought of her throwing hers away.

She dropped her package onto his lap. "What's this?" he asked.

"Aspirin. You have to have a prize of a headache, after that crack your skull got last night. You haven't complained, but you have to be hurting."

"Do I?" Actually he hadn't been hurting at all, not from the crack on his skull, not from using unexpected muscles when he split Carrie's firewood. Maybe coming back had its own strange blessings.

Before he knew what she'd planned, she reached out and touched his forehead, brushing back the too-long hair, and her hand was as gentle, and even more sensual, than when she'd stroked her car. "It's healing nicely," she said. "In a couple of days you won't even know you've hurt yourself." Her fingers still lingered, warm against his cool flesh. "Unless you cut your hair, of course."

"I was thinking of that."

"Don't you dare." She started to pull her hand away, but he caught her wrist, stopping her with gentle force.

Her eyes met his with startled wonder. "Why shouldn't I cut my hair, Carrie?"

"Maybe you should," she said breezily, not tugging at her hand. "You're a little too beautiful as it is."

His mouth curved in a wry smile. "It won't work."

"What won't work?" She yanked her hand away, and he let her go.

"You keep talking to me as if you're my maiden aunt."

"For one thing, I feel like your maiden aunt," she said with asperity. "For another..."

"For another?" he prompted.

Jeffie chose that moment to interfere. "Yeah, Carrie? For another what?"

"For another thing, I'm saving myself for you, Jeffie," she said cheerfully, starting the car. This time she didn't stroke the dashboard and croon to it. A good thing, too. He would have caught her hand in his again.

The town of Angel Falls was no more than a block long, with a diner, two gas stations, a bar, and a general store beside the pharmacy. Beneath the rapidly melting snow things looked very clean, very shabby, very depressed. It was a town on its way out but putting up a brave front nonetheless. The tatty, sparkling Christmas decorations were going up all around them.

"Isn't it a little early for Christmas decorations?" he asked.

He could sense Carrie's shoulders relaxing as he changed the subject. "It's a hard life up here," she said. "We have to celebrate anything we can. At least we wait till Thanksgiving. I know some places that start the Christmas season in mid-October."

"Like New York City."

She looked at him in surprise. "Did you used to live in New York? You don't seem the type."

"I don't know if there is a type." He avoided answering her question, turning to stare at the scenery. Half the vehicles they passed were pickup trucks, few of them newer than his. "This is a pretty poor town."

"Do tell. Ever since the mill closed down things have been pretty lean. A lot of people have moved out."

"But you moved back."

She didn't ask him how he knew. "I had no place else to go. The same with most of the people left around here. If they had a choice, they'd be gone."

He glanced around at the shabby, yet neat Victorian houses beneath their soggy blanket of snow. "I can see why. It's depressing."

"Not really. This town, and the people in it, grow on you. It's really very beautiful. But people have to make a living, and the summer people don't provide enough of an income for the whole town."

"It sounds like the whole town is in need of a miracle," he said.

"You don't have to sound so gloomy. No one's expecting you to provide it," Carrie said.

He looked at the old houses and narrow streets, and wondered whether that was true. Or whether he really was supposed to save the whole damned town.

The Swensen house was as big, or bigger, than the other old Victorian houses. The paint was peeling, but the woodwork was in perfect shape. Lars was standing on the broad front porch, wearing a flannel shirt and wool vest, hanging a Christmas wreath entwined with dried flowers and pinecones.

He pumped Gabriel's hand enthusiastically when he reached the porch, and there was no doubting the sincerity of his welcome, even to a man like Gabriel, who was used to doubting everything. "Good to see you, Gabriel," he boomed. "Maggie's already made up your room, and there's fresh coffee and bread in the kitchen." He leaned past him and gave Carrie a loud kiss on the cheek. "Some for you, too, little pigeon. We need to fatten you up."

"Bah, humbug," said Carrie with unimpaired good humor. "Jeffie will take you up on your offer. Teenage boys never stop eating."

"Aw, Carrie..." Jeffie protested, heading straight past everyone, presumably in the direction of the kitchen and food.

"Nice wreath," Gabriel murmured. Indeed, it was a piece of rare beauty, fashioned of blue spruce, the muted colors of the dried flowers complementing the greeny blue of the pine needles.

"He's been disapproving of all the decorations," Carrie piped up. "He thinks it's too early in the run room."

"Don't you be putting words in his mouth," Lars said. "We put our wreaths up at Thanksgiving, and we leave 'em up until the needles drop off and they're brown, usually sometime in April."

"Why?" Gabriel couldn't keep from asking.

"To remind us that we should all have a bit of the Christmas spirit the year round," Lars said simply. "It's a lesson we all need to learn."

"Amen," Carrie said.

Gabriel tensed, waiting in fearful anticipation for one of them to burst into prayer, but that seemed to be enough for a moment. "Come along in," Lars said, stamping the loose snow off his feet. "And I'll see if I can roust Maggie."

The inside of the house matched the exterior. It was spotless and for a moment Gabriel paused. He'd always kept his own apartment pin-neat, with the help of an overpriced cleaning service, but it had never felt like this. Somehow cozy, homey, despite the neatness. The wallpaper was faded, but the woodwork on the curving stair was smooth and polished. The runner was unraveling on top of the shining oak floorboards, and the place smelled of lemon wax and coffee and cinnamon.

"This is what heaven should smell like," he surprised himself by saying.

"I imagine it does," Lars replied, pushing open the swinging door into the huge kitchen that was the heart of the house, the heart of the family. Maggie was sitting in an old rocker near the wood cookstove, nursing the baby, a cracked mug of coffee on the table close at hand.

She raised her head and smiled, and her careworn face looked as smooth and beautiful as a Madonna's. Gabriel could feel the instinctive flush rise to his face, his desperate need to escape watching her nurse.

But there was no way he could do so gracefully. He had no choice but to let Lars show him to a seat at the wide table and plunk a mug of coffee and a couple of fresh cinnamon rolls in front of him. He stared, with rapt concentration on the rich brown of his coffee, while Lars and Carrie made appreciative noises about tiny Anna Caroline Swensen.

"She's an absolute beauty, isn't she?" Lars boomed when his guest hadn't joined in with the appropriate praise.

"Gorgeous," Gabriel said, staring at his half-eaten cinnamon roll as if it held the answers to the universe. As indeed it might. It was good enough to cure cancer.

Carrie rose abruptly, and he realized in his acute embarrassment he hadn't even been aware that she was sitting close beside him. "Do you mind if I show Gabriel his room?"

Lars waved one burly arm. "Be my guest. It's the back bedroom under the eaves. We thought it would give him the most privacy. Want to go out to the shop, Jeffie?"

Jeffie rose from the table, his mouth still full of cinnamon bun. "You bet."

"Meet us out there," Lars said. "Carrie will show you the way."

Gabriel followed Carrie in complete silence, up the narrow, winding back stairway from the kitchen. Her blond hair hung halfway down her back this morning—she hadn't bothered to do anything more than tie it with a strip of material. A piece that matched the quilt he'd slept under, he realized suddenly.

She opened a burled walnut door and stepped into the room, surveying it with satisfaction. "This is where you'll be," she said. "There's a bathroom down the hall that you'll share with Lars and Harald, and around here you need to conserve hot water, cold water, electricity and heat." She moved forward, into the room, touching the old bird's-eye maple dresser. "They moved this in for you. Lars must approve of you."

It was a beautiful piece of furniture, the only beauty the bare room had to show. The bed was a narrow metal one with a sagging mattress, utilitarian white sheets and an old gray blanket. The one window looked out over the chilly gray landscape, and the chair and table looked extremely uncomfortable.

"It's very nice," he murmured, closing the door behind them, closing them in the room.

It was a small room. She was not a tiny woman, but he was a very tall man, and the room felt crowded, by the two of them, by the sensual awareness he couldn't escape as he looked down at her.

He knew if he lifted his hands they'd be trembling with the need to touch her. In his short, misspent life he'd never felt so quintessentially alive as he did now, standing so close to her he could feel the heat from her body, could breathe in the flowery scent from her skin. He wanted her with a desperation that was an ache in his bones, and he knew he couldn't have her.

She smiled up at him, and for a moment he thought she was serene and untouched by his burning need. Until he looked into her eyes at the troubled shadow that burned beneath the bright blue. He could see the rapid flutter of pulse at the base of her throat, the faint color in her skin. He could see the hardness of her nipples through the soft cotton top, and the room was toasty warm.

She took a step back, one that seemed perfectly natural, but he wasn't fooled. She was even more wary of him than he was of her.

"You should be comfortable here. As soon as you get used to Maggie."

The change of subject, even though the other was unspoken, startled him. "What?"

"How could you have reached the age of thirty-something and not seen a woman nurse a baby?" she asked, her voice a gentle tease.

"I've done my best to avoid it," he said gruffly.

"It's only natural."

"So is death. That doesn't mean I have to like it."

"You'll get used to it," she said serenely. "Won't you want your wife to breast-feed your children?"

"I don't have a wife."

"But you will someday."

"No."

He'd shocked her. "Why not?"

He was letting too much out. He shrugged. "I just can't imagine it. What about you?"

"I don't intend to have a wife," she said with an impish smile.

"What about babies and breast-feeding?"

He'd pushed enough to get a reaction, and he saw the pain and denial darkening her eyes. "That's none of your business."

"But my reproductive plans are yours?" he countered.

"You're right, I've been too nosy. It's a failing of mine."

She obviously wasn't going to have babies any more than he was. Not unless he could make a miracle. He looked at her and wondered what kind of miracle she needed. Whether he could put his hands on her and somehow cure her.

For the moment he was afraid to try. If he touched her he wouldn't be content with comfort, with healing. If he touched her he'd try to draw her down onto that narrow, sagging bed. And despite, or perhaps because of, her wariness, he knew there was a good chance she'd go with him.

He took a step back away from her, noting without comment the relief in her eyes. "That's all right," he said. "When I make my plans about babies you'll be the first to know."

And suddenly the relief vanished, leaving only the beginnings of an impossible longing. Impossible for both of them. And he started thinking that even the other place might be easier than this one. And a woman he couldn't touch.

Chapter Five

"You don't talk much, do you?" Lars Swensen was leaning over a piece of cherry-colored wood, running a strip of sandpaper down the edge with the tenderness of a mother smoothing her child's hair.

"No," Gabriel said, picking up a block of wood that someone, probably Lars, had begun carving and then abandoned.

"Well, I'm used to that. In case you hadn't guessed, I'm from Scandinavian stock myself, and most Swedes aren't much in the talking department. Course, Maggie says I make up for my family. I like a little conversation now and then."

"You won't get idle chatter from me." Gabriel leaned one hip on the high stool and picked up a tiny chisel.

"I don't need idle chatter. The shop gets lonely here. I'd appreciate the company, even if you don't want to talk. Though you strike me as a man who'd have a lot to say, given the right circumstances."

The wood felt rich, alive beneath Gabriel's rough fingertips. "I don't know what those circumstances would be," he said absently, digging a little bit into the wood with the razor-sharp chisel.

"You done much work with carving? That piece was part of the nativity scene I was doing for the church. I've done most of it, and then I get stuck. You know they talk about writer's block? Well, carpenters get it, too, sometimes. I've wasted more wood, trying to carve the rest of the figures."

Gabriel snicked off another chip of wood. "What have you got left to do?"

"I've done the holy family with no problem at all. I've got the shepherds and the wise men just about finished. But no matter how hard I try I can't carve the angels."

The chisel slipped, slicing into Gabriel's hand, and he dropped the block of wood back onto the workbench. "Really?" he said mildly enough, staring at the bright red blood welling from the shallow gash on his knuckle.

"Maybe you could give it a try," Lars continued, still concentrating on his block of cherry.

"Angels aren't my thing," Gabriel said.

Lars looked up then, obviously struck by something in his voice. "All right," he said finally. "But feel free to play around with it. I'm certainly not getting anywhere."

For a moment Gabriel's hands stilled as he stared at the wood. He knew nothing about carving, nothing about tools. And yet the plain block of wood had begun to take on a form. Not much of one, and yet he could see it clearly beneath the rough texture of the block of fine-grained cherry. The wings were delicately etched, widespread in silent flight. The face was calm, with an almost unearthly beauty. It was the face of the stranger he'd seen in the mirror.

He put the block down on the bench. "Maybe later," he said, and he could hear the strain in his deep voice.

She was standing behind him. He knew it without looking, without hearing, knew it with an instinct as certain as it was frightening. He didn't understand the effect she had on him, the feeling of destiny. And why couldn't he have felt it before, in another lifetime for both of them? Or had he?

He turned slowly, filling his eyes with her. She was standing silhouetted in the doorway, the baby in her arms, and he stared for a moment, wishing he could see a happy ending for her. Wishing he could see babies and health and a future, just as he'd seen the angel in the block of wood. But all he could see was a woman with a sorrow so deep and so eternal that no miracle of his could change it.

"Believe it or not, I'm going to the mall," she announced, her cheerful voice both startling and yet completely believable. "Maggie and I can't believe the Christmas season is really starting unless we partake of that madness, at least vicariously, so you've got the baby for the afternoon."

"I wanted to get some work done," Lars protested, reaching out for the child with welcoming arms despite his grumbling.

"It's the day after Thanksgiving. No one needs to work then."

"They do if they want to get the crèche ready by the first Sunday in Advent."

"You've got all of Saturday," she said. "Besides, you need Mary, Joseph and a donkey to start out with, right? You've already finished those."

"And an angel," he said morosely. "Don't forget the angel."

"Gabriel can do it. He's got the right name for it."

She wasn't looking at him, and he knew it was deliberate. He wasn't even surprised by her suggestion. If he questioned her she'd doubtless simply make a joke of it. But despite common sense, he knew there was a connection between the two of them, one she felt just as strongly as he did. The difference was, she didn't know what was behind it.

"You've got your choice, Gabriel," Lars said cheerfully, beaming down at his baby daughter. "You can hold the baby, or you can see what you can do for an angel. Carrie's right—we need one for Sunday morning. Mary, Joseph and the donkey start in the rear window of the church, heading toward Bethlehem. We need an angel waiting at the stable over on top of the organ."

For a moment Gabriel didn't move, once again certain he'd stumbled into a group of religious fanatics at the very least, or perhaps one of those extremely weird cults. Neither Lars nor Carrie seemed the slightest bit fanatical about it, however, merely matter-of-fact and almost alarmingly cheerful about the whole thing.

"What will happen if you don't have the angel? Does God strike you dead, or something?" he drawled, his hand drifting toward the piece of wood that held the angel imprisoned inside.

"Nope," Carrie said. "We'll use our imagination. Or maybe dredge up the battered papier-mâché angel from the Sunday school crèche." Her eyes narrowed as she looked at his hands, and she took a sudden step toward him. "You've cut yourself," she said, putting her small, delicate hands over his.

He looked down at them, at her hands on top of his large, strong ones, and for a moment he said nothing, feeling the life flowing through her into him. "Just a scratch," he said, and indeed, the blood had stopped.

"Let me get you a bandage...."

Gently he removed his hands from her grasp, and she released him, stepping back. "It's fine," he said. "Go shopping, and I'll see what I can do about an angel."

It was the wrong thing to say. Her eyes lit up, and she looked like a child who'd been given a new pony for Christmas. He didn't want to bring her that much joy. He wanted to save her life, right whatever wrongs he'd done her, and then leave her to some other man to live happily ever after with. Didn't he? His eyes met hers, and something danced between them, a current of feeling with a life all its own. He wanted to pull back, needed to pull back, and yet he couldn't. All he could do was stand there, watching her.

Carrie hadn't moved, staring at him, entranced. "Get a move on, girlie," Lars boomed, and the baby in his arms jumped at the sudden sound of his voice. "If you and Maggie intend to buy anything more than sore feet and a headache, you'd better get started. Let's leave the man in peace and see what he can come up with. This little girl needs changing, I need some coffee and doughnuts."

The moment passed almost as if that thread of silent communication had never happened. "We won't be too long," Carrie said, backing away, her eyes still lingering.

"Promises, promises," Lars grumbled cheerfully. "We'll probably see you a few hours before Saint Lucia's Day."

"That's part of why we're going. You know who the oldest girl is this year," Carrie said, her attention finally off Gabriel.

He could feel some of the tension ease from him. As long as she watched him, concentrated on him, he felt intensely, painfully alive. He preferred the dull cocoon of life he'd been existing in. Except it hadn't been life, had it?

"What's Saint Lucia's Day?" he asked anyway, knowing it would bring her eyes, her attention back to him, unable to resist.

"You don't know Saint Lucia? Then again, I don't suppose she's much of a Catholic saint. The Scandinavians have pretty much taken her over," Carrie said.

For a moment he was about to deny his implied Catholic heritage, then wisely closed his mouth. He was Gabriel Falconi from the North End of Boston. He couldn't be anything but Catholic.

"We've got a lot of saints," he muttered. "I always liked Saint Jude."

"Patron of lost causes? The people in Angel Falls know a lot about that," Lars said. "You'll like Saint Lucia's Day, Gabriel. The oldest girl gets to wear a crown of candles and a white dress and serve cake to everyone."

"It doesn't sound like much of a holiday to me," he drawled.

"Wait till you taste the cakes." Lars patted his own estimable stomach beneath the comfortable burden of the baby. "You're going to have the best Christmas season of your life."

Gabriel glanced over at Carrie. "I have no doubt of that whatsoever," he said evenly.

And Carrie blushed.

MAGGIE SLID back in the passenger seat of Carrie's old car, closing her eyes for a moment. "I shouldn't be doing this," she said. "I'm behind on the laundry, Nils needs help with his algebra, Lars needs to work on the crèche, not watch the baby."

"You can't take care of all the people all the time," Carrie said in her most reasonable tone of voice.

Maggie turned her head and looked at her, a faint ghost of amusement in her weary eyes. "You might listen to your own advice. You're running yourself ragged."

"Oh, a perfect saint I am," she mocked, uncomfortable. "You know perfectly well I don't have half the demands on my life that you have."

"You only wish you did."

The image of baby Carrie hit her hard, sneaking up on her as it did so often. "Well, I don't. And won't, for that matter. I told you, I'm not cut out for a family and kids. Look on the bright side, Maggie. I can come and get my baby-longing taken care of by a good solid dose of your kids, and it gives you a break at the same time. It works out very well for both of us."

"Not that well for you. I just wish . . ."

"I just wish we didn't have to talk about it," Carrie said firmly. "It's the beginning of the Christmas season. Let's think about what we can afford to buy."

"Not much," Maggie said in her gloomiest voice.

"What is this, *The Grinch Who Stole Christmas?* We can always come up with enough for a sack of peppermints, and what could be more Christmassy? I think our finances can spread to some new hair ribbons for Kirsten, maybe even some gold stars for her Saint Lucia crown. You were going to get some yarn for a new work sweater for Lars, one he can wear in the woods."

Wrong subject, Carrie thought, as Maggie's face crumpled in sudden grief. "I'm frightened, Carrie. So very frightened. The woods are dangerous, and you know as well as I do that Hunsicker runs a sloppy operation. If two of his men hadn't been injured there'd be no work for Lars."

It was an old worry, one that Carrie had tried to calm innumerable times. It was hard work, soothing Maggie's fears, when Carrie knew how reasonable they were.

"We just have to trust, Maggie. Too many bad things have happened in the past few years, since the mill closed down. It's only natural to expect more disasters to follow, but they're not going to. Lars is a careful worker, and he keeps his tools in top shape. He's not going to get hurt...."

"You're right," Maggie said abruptly. "Let's not talk about gloomy things. We can't do anything but get depressed, and Christmas isn't the time for depression. Let's talk about something more cheerful."

"Like what?" Carrie asked warily.

"Like Gabriel Falconi. Pretty cute, isn't he?"

"I wouldn't call him cute."

"What would you call him? Don't try to pretend you haven't noticed what a hunk he is. He's the best-looking thing I've seen since Lars."

"Maggie!" Carrie said in mock horror. "And here I thought you and Lars were the perfect couple."

"Don't try to mislead me. You've got your eye on him. I see a romance in your future."

"I don't have my eye on anyone. I'm not interested in romance, and well you know it." She could hear the strain in her voice, and her hopeless longing hung heavy in the air—there was no disguising it with her oldest friend.

"Whoever he was, Carrie, he's not worth spending the rest of your life as a nun," Maggie said sternly. "Gabriel is here, he's gorgeous, unattached, obviously heterosexual...."

"What makes you assume that?" Carrie gave in to her curiosity.

"I've seen the way he looks at you when he thinks no one is looking."

It shouldn't hurt, Carrie thought distantly. It shouldn't feel like a spear in her belly, the ache spreading outward through her body in a white-hot heat. She'd shut off her feelings, her vulnerability, content to be a wise mother superior, spreading asexual kindness around her like alms for the poor. She'd told herself her heart was buried with the cold son of a bitch she'd fallen in love with in New York, and it worked best for her to believe it. But now, in the space of less than twenty-four hours, her life had been turned upside down again, and all by the dark-eyed gaze of a man who looked like a fallen angel.

"You're imagining it," she said flatly.

"I am not. Every time you walk into the room the intensity level rises ten degrees. He—"

"We're going to end up either furious with each other or in tears by the time we reach the mall," Carrie interrupted. "Wanna talk about recipes?" She got in line behind a motorcade of shoppers heading into the newly built mall on the outskirts of Saint Luke, the closest thing to a city their area of Minnesota boasted.

For a moment Maggie didn't say a word. Then she reached out and put her work-worn hand on Carrie's. "I like to use a trace of cardamom in my sugar cookie recipe."

Carrie flashed her a grateful smile. "Cardamom's fine, if you don't use too heavy a hand."

"Then again, coriander adds a nice touch."

"I can never tell the difference. My heavens, a parking place!" Carrie gasped. "Do you suppose this is a sign from God?"

"To get a parking spot right near the entrance? Absolutely. We're going to have the best Christmas ever."

GABRIEL SET the half-finished angel down on the battered workbench and stared at it in wonder. It was late afternoon, and he'd been alone in Lars's shop for uncounted hours, stopping only when Lars would appear carrying apple pie and strong Scandinavian coffee. The first hour he'd sat alone, staring at the block of wood as he tried to figure out how to use the tiny chisels. The more he'd concentrated the more he'd fouled up. When Lars made his first appearance after putting the baby down for a nap, he hadn't said a word about the carving. He'd simply left the food, turned on the tiny radio and left.

Gabriel had drunk the coffee, devoured the pie with more appetite than he'd ever remembered, and listened to the music. Christmas music already, he told himself in disgust. And yet, as he listened to the music and thought about all the reasons he shouldn't be enjoying some new-age rendition of "Good King Wenceslas," his hands picked up the piece of cherry and began to work.

Each time he stopped to think about it his hands would become clumsy. He'd never been a slow learner, and obviously the part of him that was Gabriel Falconi was equally adept. If he thought about it he wouldn't know what he was doing. So he concentrated on the music, on the soothing, flowing sounds, and let his hands do the thinking for him.

"Fine work."

He hadn't heard Lars come in. The older man stood beside him, looking down at the angel. "You've got a real gift," Lars continued. "And I'm the man to recognize it, if I may say so without false modesty. She's a real beauty, she is. You've got the touch."

Gabriel looked down at his hands. They were nicked, scratched, big and clumsy looking to his unaccustomed eyes. "I guess I do," he murmured.

"She reminds me of someone," Lars said, lifting the figurine. "Something about her face that I can't quite place. She's a regular tartar, isn't she?"

Gabriel looked down into Augusta's stern, judgmental face. "She is that."

"You wouldn't think of an angel being quite such an old grump, would you? She'd scare the bejesus out of me if I had to face her on judgment day. And yet she looks just right." He clapped a hand on Gabriel's shoulder and squeezed it. "Just right," he said again.

Gabriel looked at him. In his previous incarnation he might have thought that was mild praise. But the man he'd become was more sensitive than his old self. And Lars Swensen had given him high praise, indeed.

"Thanks," he said. "I'll finish her up tomorrow and do the other one. If you want me to, that is. It took me a while to get started."

Lars nodded. "It does, sometimes. It was worth the wait. What do you see for the other one? Another judge?"

Gabriel stared down at Augusta's dry-humored face. "I'm not sure," he said slowly. "I'll have to see what my hands come up with."

An energetic wail emerged from the house. "Someone's calling. The women haven't returned from shopping yet, so I suppose we'd better see what we can rustle up. How are you in the cooking department?"

He thought of the cooking courses de rigueur for an upscale bachelor. Somehow he didn't think Lars would appreciate slivers of raw octopus ringed with duck pâté ravioli. "I can cook," he said. "Steak and spaghetti."

"Sounds my speed. Except this is the day after Thanksgiving. It's un-American to eat anything but turkey hash."

"Turkey hash?"

"Good Lord, are they that uncivilized in Boston? You haven't lived until you've eaten real turkey hash. Prepare yourself for a culinary feast."

"What culinary feast, Pop?" Nils demanded when they stepped into the blast furnace of a kitchen. Gabriel hadn't realized how chilly the shop was, so intent on his work that he hadn't allowed any conscious thought to enter.

"Turkey hash."

"Gross," Nils replied emphatically.

"Yuck," said Kirsten as she rhythmically pounded the baby's back.

"What a thing to do to a perfectly decent turkey," Nils added. "Couldn't we just have turkey sandwiches?"

"You had them for lunch. Besides, Carrie bought a turkey the size of Minneapolis. Food is too precious to waste."

"How about tacos, Pop? We've got some ground beef in the freezer."

"Turkey enchiladas." For a moment Gabriel didn't realize the words had come from his own mouth.

"Say what?" Nils demanded suspiciously.

"I make turkey enchiladas." He might as well carry through with it. If he could carve something that looked fiendishly like his nemesis, Augusta, then he could probably make turkey enchiladas, as well. He'd never been fond of Mexican food. And yet suddenly he had a craving as fierce as that of any woman eight months pregnant. He wanted something rife with chili powder and tortillas, and if he had to use turkey and cook it himself to get it, then he would.

"Sounds great to me. What do you need?"

For a moment Gabriel drew a blank. Shutting his eyes, he went into that blank deliberately. "Tortillas, chili powder, tomato sauce, jack cheese and onions."

"I'll go to the store," Nils shouted.

"Not by yourself, you won't. You only have a learner's permit. I'll drive, and we'll stop and pick up Jeffie. He's alone too much as it is." Lars turned to Gabriel. "You don't mind holding down the fort, do you? Kirsten can handle the little ones."

It wasn't panic, Gabriel told himself. It was his sheer dislike of children. He'd always found them noisy, messy creatures, and he didn't want to be trapped with three of them, alone. Except that Lars's children were the exception. Kirsten was bright, pretty, sweet tempered. The younger boy, whatever his name was, had a mischievous smile that somehow reached past Gabriel's natural reserve. And even the baby had something about her that was far too appealing.

He'd survive. "Take your time," he said grandly, pouring himself another cup of that wickedly strong coffee. And he didn't regret his words for another twenty-three minutes.

Chapter Six

It was snowing by the time Carrie and Maggie pulled into the steep driveway outside the Swensen home. The roads had gotten slick enough to make any normal amount of speed unwise, and for once Carrie had listened to her better judgment. She didn't like the fact that she wanted to get back to the Swensens', wanted to with something close to desperation. Because she knew perfectly well what it was she was trying to get back to. Something she didn't deserve and wasn't going to have.

"Do you suppose they were worried about us?" Maggie asked as she climbed out of the front seat, her arms laden with packages.

"Probably. Do you care?"

"Not enough to come back any sooner," she admitted. "I bet they're sitting around, grumpy, expecting me to cook them dinner."

"I thought Lars was above that sort of thing."

"Honey, no man is above that sort of thing. They all expect you to wait on them hand and foot, even the best of them."

"Lars being one of the best of them?"

"Absolutely," Maggie panted, struggling up the icy driveway. "I haven't decided how Gabriel stacks up in the hierarchy of perfect men."

"Lars being a ten?" Carrie took several of the bulky packages from Maggie's icy hands.

"I imagine Gabriel might be somewhere near a four," Maggie said thoughtfully.

Carrie's protest was immediate, instinctive and unvoiced. "You can't get me to rise to the bait, Maggie. For all we know he could be a minus three."

"Not when he looks like that. I'll give him four points just for looks alone. It's a good thing Angel Falls is singularly devoid of unattached women. You won't have any competition."

"Maggie," she warned, stamping her snowy feet on the sturdy front porch.

"Not that you should worry about competition anyway. Any man worth his salt would choose you over an entire herd of Miss America contestants." She pushed open the door, and heat and light flooded out onto the porch.

"What's this about Miss America contestants?" Lars's voice boomed out as his sturdy frame filled the kitchen doorway.

"No such luck, sweetheart. You've got me," Maggie said.

"And you've brought half the stores in Saint Luke back with you." There was no missing the worry in his voice. "I thought we'd decided we couldn't afford much of a Christmas."

"Don't give your wife grief," Carrie said, shutting the door behind her. "She spent a pittance. Just be glad we came home to feed you...." Her voice trailed off as she sniffed the air. "What's cooking?"

"That doesn't smell like turkey hash," Maggie said in an accusing voice.

"It's not. It's turkey enchiladas, and it's only by the magnanimous goodness of my soul and the Christmas spirit that I managed to save enough for you two."

"You've never made enchiladas."

"I still haven't. Gabriel's the chef." He reached out for the packages. "I'll hide these. You two go in and get something to eat before you waste away to skin and bones."

"Impossible for me," Maggie said with a sigh, hanging her coat on a hook, "and too late for Carrie."

"It's never too late for Carrie," Lars said firmly, giving the women a little shove.

The kitchen was empty. Maggie looked around her in dismay. "I'm not sure it's worth it," she said as she surveyed the pile of dishes in the sink, the pots and pans littering every spare surface of the kitchen she'd left spotless.

"Lars said he was a chef, not a scullery maid," Carrie pointed out, heading for the sink. "I'll just get a start on these..."

"Oh, no, you won't." Lars was back in record time. "You sit down and I'll serve you." He scooped a pile of dishes off the table, dumped them into the sink and turned with a fatuous smile. "You won't believe what you're tasting. I didn't know leftover turkey had such possibilities."

"I don't believe what I'm seeing," Maggie said tartly.

"Neither do I," Carrie echoed softly, sinking down in surprise onto the chair Lars held for her.

Gabriel was standing in the doorway. The mess from creating his culinary masterpiece hadn't left him untouched. Chili sauce adorned his eyebrow, spattered his chambray shirt and stained his jeans. But that wasn't the most surprising thing about him. In his arms rested little Carrie Swensen, cooing cheerfully, equally bedaubed in that evening's dinner.

"Baby!" Maggie cried, reaching out for her younger daughter. "Little Anna Caroline."

For a moment the baby was torn. "I'm not sure she'll go to you, sweetheart," Lars said, placing two overfilled plates in front of them. "I think she's in love."

Gabriel's face was a study in contradictions. On the one hand, he seemed supremely embarrassed at the baby's obvious adoration. On the other, there was a surprising competence in the way he held her, as if those arms were used to babies, despite his earlier insistence that he had never even seen a woman nurse.

"She got upset when Lars and Nils went to the store," Gabriel said in his deep, slow voice. "I just managed to calm her."

Carrie could imagine it. She'd seen the baby when she was in one of her tears, and it was not a pretty sight. Usually nothing outside of her mother's arms could calm her, but Gabriel seemed possessed of a magic touch. Maybe lying in his arms, listening to that deep voice rumble through his chest...

She dropped her fork with a noisy clatter.

"What's the matter?" Gabriel asked. "Don't you like my cooking?"

She looked up, meeting his dark, enigmatic eyes over the baby's curly head. It was flirtation, a mild, clumsy form of it that seemed to surprise him as much as it surprised her. "It's wonderful," she said truthfully. "I just never got in the habit of eating much."

"I keep telling her she's too thin," Maggie said, her fork scraping against her now-empty plate. "Tell her she's too thin, Gabriel."

"She's too thin," he said in that slow, deep voice of his.

It took all of Carrie's concentration, but she managed to shake off the slumberous effect of it. "Well," she said briskly, "I'll just have to be a disappointment to you all. Even if I ate twice as much, I wouldn't put on weight. My metabolism isn't geared toward comfortable curves."

"You'd think she'd be proud of it," Maggie mourned. "Are there any more enchiladas?"

"Nope," Lars said.

"Are you going to finish yours?" She cast a covetous eye at Carrie's barely touched plate.

"Yes, she is," Gabriel said, handing Maggie the baby and moving to loom over Carrie.

He'd flirted with her, maybe, just maybe, she could flirt back a little. What harm would it do? "What'll you give me if I do?"

He was too close to her. Maggie had risen, resigned to her empty plate, and Gabriel took her vacated seat, next to Carrie. "Dessert," he said.

Carrie just stared at him, visions of all sorts of things, none of them sugarplums, dancing in her head.

She opened her mouth to say something, then shut it again, pushing the still-full plate away from her, pushing her empty heart away from her. "Not for me. I'd better get back home. The roads are slick and my stove's probably out by now."

"Spend the night," Lars suggested. "It's too nasty a night to drive all that way by yourself."

"My pipes will freeze, and I can't afford a plumber. Besides, that's what I got the car for. Don't worry about me, Lars. I'll be fine."

"I do worry about you, Carrie. We all do," Lars said earnestly, leaning over the table between them.

"Don't." The word was short, raw, the pain obvious to anyone attuned to it. She didn't deserve their concern.

"At least let me follow you back and make sure you get home safely...."

"No."

"Gabriel can follow you," Maggie piped up, keeping her attention on her daughter so that she couldn't meet Carrie's glare. "He can make sure your stove is going before he leaves."

"No," she said again. "I can take care of myself, and well you know it." She rose, not meeting Gabriel's dark, steady gaze. "But if you'd like to come out tomorrow and look over the work I have for you..."

"Tonight would be better for me," he said.

She thought he'd missed the byplay. "Why?" she asked flatly.

"Because tomorrow I have to finish one carving and do another, I promised Lars I'd take the stuff down to the church, and I wanted to check on my truck. It's tonight or next week."

"Next week would be just fine...."

"Give it up, Carrie," Maggie said. "The man wants to come tonight, let him come tonight. Let somebody do something for you for a change."

There was nothing she could do, short of causing a scene. Lars and Maggie were the best people in the world, but they might have invented the phrase "stubborn Swedes." And if truth be told, she wasn't sure that she wanted to drive on the slick surface of the long twisting road. Four-wheel drive was all well and good, but not when it came to glare ice.

"All right, I'm not going to keep fighting," she said wearily. "All I want to do is go home and go to bed. If you insist that Gabriel follow me to make sure I get there safely then I'm sure I can't stop you, even though there's absolutely no need. But I'm tired, I don't want to drag Gabriel all over the house in an ice storm showing him what needs fixing. He can follow me home, watch me get safely inside the house, and then go home. Satisfied?"

"Satisfied," Lars said. "Take my pickup, Gabe. She's old and rusty but she runs like a top, and you're going to need the four-wheel drive on a night like this." He turned to Carrie. "Sit yourself back down, have some dessert and a cup of coffee before you go out into the night."

Part of her would have killed for coffee, but the longer she delayed getting home the more she'd be playing into the Swensens' heavy-handed matchmaking. Besides, she was exhausted. She needed to collapse in her own bed as soon as possible, and accepting

Gabriel's help was the path that would lead her home the quickest.

"No coffee, no dessert."

"No coffee?" Lars echoed, horrified. "Some sherry, then? Something to warm your bones."

"A kiss good-night," she said, leaning over and kissing his burly cheek. "I'll get you both for this," she whispered in his ear.

Lars didn't look the slightest bit chastened. "Don't do anything I wouldn't do."

Gabriel followed her out into the hall, Lars's keys in his hand, an unreadable expression on his face. She braced herself, waiting for him to make some comment, but he was silent, looming over her. He didn't help her on with her coat, a wise move on his part. She was already in a bad mood, having to accept help when she was the one who wanted to offer it, and if he'd been fool enough to be oversolicitous she would have lashed out at him, she who seldom said a harsh word to a living soul other than herself.

But he didn't say a word, didn't try to touch her, simply waited as she struggled into her coat, and she reminded herself she was being paranoid. He didn't know a thing about her and her myriad problems. No one knew all her problems, or the depths of the harm she'd done. No one needed to know. Her own conscience was punishment enough.

"You don't need to do this, you know," she said. "Lars and Maggie are overprotective. I've been driving these roads since I was sixteen, usually without the benefit of four-wheel drive or even snow tires."

"They care about you."

"A little too much, if you ask me."

"I didn't know that was possible," Gabriel said.

It was useless to argue. "It's fairly direct to my house—you shouldn't have any trouble retracing the path, unless you have no sense of direction."

An odd expression flashed into his eyes. "I don't know," he said simply.

She didn't stop to consider the ramifications of that statement. "Well, I guess you'll find out tonight, won't you? Have you done much winter driving?"

"Last night," he said, the faint trace of a smile curving his mouth.

God, she loved his mouth. Immediately she slapped down that thought. "That's not much of a testimonial."

"It was a fluke. I'll be fine."

"I don't want to be pulling you out of a ditch. Maybe you ought to stay home."

He took her arm. Major mistake, she thought. She liked the feel of his hand on her arm, strong, forceful without being bullying, protective. She didn't let people protect her, she was too busy protecting them. But, Lord, it felt good, if only for a brief, self-indulgent moment.

"I think," he said, "that we ought to stop arguing and get on the roads before they become impassable. Assuming you haven't changed your mind and decided to spend the night here?"

"I haven't changed my mind." He still hadn't released her arm, and not for a moment was she tempted to yank it free. "I hope I made myself clear—I want you to stay in the truck until I'm safely in the house and then drive straight back home."

He didn't answer. Instead, he opened the door, letting a blast of damp, icy air into the house. "Let's go," he said.

And since his warm, strong hand was still clasped around her upper arm, she had no choice but to follow.

GABRIEL DROVE SLOWLY, following behind her on the icy roads as he considered his course of action. He was glad to see some sign of temper in her. He'd begun to think of her as the saint of Angel Falls. A hell of a combination, he thought with a sour smile. A saint, and a broken-down angel. He was the one who was supposed to be the good one, wasn't he?

He wasn't sure of anything anymore. There were times when he felt like Gabriel Falconi, comfortable and familiar inside a strange body, a strange head. Emerson Wyatt MacVey III was a dream, someone he'd read about in a book. Not a very good book, at that. One of those depressing anti-yuppie novels he'd struggled through in a previous life.

He concentrated on the red taillights ahead of him. Lars was right, the truck held the icy road fairly well. He found he was adept at driving through bad conditions. He automatically steered into a skid, using just the right amount of pressure on the gas pedal, and took a moment to admire his expertise. The moment he did, he began to skid again, and this time he over-corrected, sliding first one way and then another on the slippery road.

He managed to pull it out of the spin, setting it back on the straight and narrow, his palms sweating, curses filling the air. Why couldn't he remember? He had all sorts of talents he never knew existed, if he just remembered to use his instincts and not his brain. If Emerson thought about driving on nightmarish roads he'd end up in a ditch. If Gabriel concentrated on the woman ahead of him and let his hands and feet, not his mind, do the driving, he'd be just fine.

He followed her up the long, twisting driveway to the dark house, watched as she turned off her car, waved goodbye in the glare of his headlights and moved toward the door with deceptive energy. He knew how tired she was, he could see the purple stains beneath her blue eyes, the paleness of her complexion, even the faint tremor in her hands. He could also see that there was no smoke coming from the chimney overhead.

He waited until the kitchen lights came on, then switched off the truck and bounded after her.

She was standing in the kitchen door, glaring at him. "I thought I told you to go home."

"Then why are you standing in the door?"

"I knew I couldn't trust you."

"Sure you can, Carrie," he said. "I'm here to see you home safely, and that's what I'm going to do. Now why don't you let me in so I can see about your wood stove instead of standing there letting more cold air inside?"

It was reasonable, but he could see by the expression on her face that she wasn't in the mood to be reasonable. He decided to take it out of her hands, pushing past her very gently and closing the door behind him.

The kitchen was icy. "Why don't you make me some coffee while I get the stove started?" he said.

"I can't."

"Why not?"

"I already checked. The water's frozen."

She was a strong woman, but her voice cracked slightly. He wanted to draw her into his arms, to warm her slender, weary body with his. He shoved his hands into his pockets to keep from touching her.

"I'll get the stove going first," he said. "Come into the living room and wrap yourself up in something while I work on it, and then I'll see what I can do about the water."

"You're a plumber?" she asked, her voice incredulous.

"Anyone can unfreeze water if the pipes haven't burst yet, and I don't think it's been that cold for that long."

"You're a man of hidden talents," she said wryly, following him meekly enough.

"I know," he said wryly.

He almost asked her to turn on the radio. Something to distract him from that intermittent clumsiness that assailed him when he least needed it. There were a few coals glowing at the bottom of the blue enamel stove, and he hummed beneath his breath as he stirred the ashes, opened the draft just the right amount and dropped only a minimal amount of kindling on it. In a moment it blazed forth, eating into the logs he placed on top of it.

"You've very good at that," Carrie said. She was curled up on the sofa where he'd slept the night before, wrapped in the quilt that had kept him warm. It was that potent, dangerous distraction that had enabled him to be so efficient with the fire. "Most people don't understand the idiosyncracies of wood stoves.''

"I have a fair amount of common sense," he said. No, I don't, his mind protested. If I did, I wouldn't be anywhere near her. Or at least I wouldn't be thinking the kind of things I'm thinking. "You got a hair dryer?"

Carrie grimaced. "Where it belongs. Under the kitchen sink, bought for the express purpose of thawing frozen pipes. Listen, don't bother. I can handle it, once I warm up. You'd better go home before the roads get any worse."

"It just kills you to accept help, doesn't it?"

"I didn't ask for help. I can manage on my own." She shivered, despite the rapidly warming temperature of the room, despite the brightly colored quilt bundled around her.

"I'm sure you can. But you helped me out yesterday. I like to repay my debts." It was the best possible thing he could have said. She couldn't accept someone's help. But she could accept someone else's need to even things up.

"All right," she said with a sigh. "If it will make you feel better."

It took him longer than he expected to get the water flowing again. As the heat from the living room stove began to filter through into the kitchen his hands began to lose their numbness, and he was finally rewarded with a sputtering, then steady, stream of water from the open faucet.

The adjoining bathroom was in worse shape. By the time he had water moving through all the fixtures he was tired, dirty and hungry. He washed one level of grime from his hands and face and headed out to the living room.

She was asleep on the sofa, her long blond hair fanned out around her pale face, her hands still clutching the quilt around her. He loaded the stove as quietly as possible, banking it down, and then squatted down beside her, watching her.

She didn't open her eyes. "Don't," she said, her lips barely moving, the sound so soft he thought he might have imagined it.

But he hadn't. "Don't what?"

"Don't look at me like that." This time she did open her eyes, staring up at him with a fearlessness he knew was completely fake. She was frightened of him, and he couldn't imagine why.

"Like what?"

"I'm not available. I'm not someone to help you while away some time spent in a high prairie town. I'm not a convenient bed partner, or even a one-night stand. I've made my life, and it's a solitary one. Don't jump to any conclusions."

"Who says I'm asking?" he demanded in a slow, deep voice, not moving.

Her pale face flooded with color. "I'm sorry," she said, her voice muffled. "I guess I was the one jumping to conclusions."

He should rise, say something friendly and walk away. And he knew he wasn't going to do that. There was a reason she was warning him away, and it wasn't just him she was afraid of. It was herself.

"No," he said. "You're not." And he leaned over and brushed her lips with his.

Chapter Seven

Sunday morning dawned still and clear, with a warm front coming through and melting the layer of snow and ice that had clung to the stubborn Minnesota earth since Thanksgiving. Gabriel arrived at the Messiah Lutheran Church with the Swensen family, all of them scrubbed and combed and spruced up. He'd had to make do with the contents of the duffel bag. There were no Italian suits, no tailored wool blazers, not even a reasonable pair of khakis. Clearly Gabriel Falconi's idea of formal dress was a pair of unpatched jeans and a fresh cotton shirt.

He'd pushed it a bit, trying to iron the wrinkles out of one of them, but apparently that bit of domestic art was beyond even the estimable Gabriel. He tried whistling, tried concentrating on the inane but funny plot of the sitcom the Swensen family had watched the night before, to no avail. His hands were clumsy, impossible as he tried to iron, and even succumbing to the ultimate distraction only led to disaster.

Carrie's lips had tasted better than anything he'd ever kissed. They'd been soft, unresisting, surprised, and it had taken a self-control he'd never known he possessed to simply brush her mouth with his, not deepen it as he'd longed to, not push her back on the couch and warm his cold body and hers with a heat that had been burning inside him since he first saw her.

But he hadn't. He'd moved away without a word, leaving her staring up at him in numb surprise, and he'd left her before she could gather her wits together.

He'd driven back home over the slick roads, remembering the feel of her mouth, and that memory hadn't been far from his mind for the past thirty-six hours, culminating with a huge triangle-shaped scorch mark on his best shirt.

He'd given up then, settling for wrinkles, but been fool enough to ask Lars for a tie. Lars had looked at him as if he were crazy, but handed him a subdued narrow tie that should have felt at home around Emerson's neck. It strangled Gabriel.

"No one wears a tie to church anymore, Gabe," Lars said kindly when he brought it back. "You won't be offending anyone. It's not going to make any difference in the eyes of God, and no one in heaven's going to care."

Gabriel thought of Augusta's flinty eyes. "You'd be surprised," he'd said glumly.

Now he stood just inside the church, surveying the congregation while the younger Swensens whispered and fought, and he thanked God he'd at least had a look at the place the day before when he'd helped Lars with the pieces of the crèche.

It was unlike any church he could remember. When he'd bothered to go to church, he'd frequented Saint Barts on Fifth Avenue and 50th Street, an old, ele-

gant church attended by all the right people. He sensed
the eyes he was looking through were more accustomed to pomp and circumstance and stained glass.
The Messiah Lutheran Church was plain, sturdy, with
maple pews, oak trim, and a huge unadorned silver
cross hanging from the front of the church. The organ was in front, and on top was a deliberately crude-
looking stable filled with straw, one of Lars's beauti-
fully carved cows, and the first angel.

Augusta perched on top of the miniature roof, arms
outspread, face stern and judgmental. He'd had
qualms about putting her right up there. The second
angel had been much more user-friendly, an adolescent male with blond curls and a vulnerable face. He
had no idea where that vision had come from. On the
surface, he was much closer to the traditional idea of
angels—sexless, pretty boys with outspread wings. It
was only when you looked closer that you could see
the fear in the wide, blank eyes.

Lars's carvings of Mary and Joseph were in a back
window, along with a donkey, starting their journey
toward Bethlehem, Lars had told him. Gabriel had
wanted to sneer at the notion. Instead, he found himself strangely moved.

There'd been no way he could get out of going to
church that day, not unless he'd asked directions to the
nearest Catholic church. And while the overt reli-
giousness of the Swensens, and indeed, everyone he'd
met in Angel Falls, made him acutely uncomfortable,
at least they didn't try to foist it upon him, and didn't
spend hours ranting. Their faith simply seemed to be
a part of their lives, just as shopping and driving cars
and eating were.

Besides, he'd kept away from Carrie Alexander quite deliberately yesterday. He wanted to give her time to think about that kiss, to see what she was going to do about it. And he wanted to give himself time to get his unaccustomed libido under control.

He'd spent the day in Lars's workshop, finishing up Augusta, carving the young man. At least Lars saw no arcane resemblance in the young man's perfect face.

The word on Gabriel's truck wasn't encouraging. Steve had hemmed and hawed and muttered about differentials and main cylinders, phrases that meant nothing to Gabriel, but the bottom line was there'd be no moving on for him, even if he'd wanted to, for at least another week.

It was still an option, he thought. Gabriel didn't have much money, but he was possessed of a gold credit card, a miracle in itself. He hadn't had a chance to check the credit limit, but he suspected he could probably manage to fly to New York and live out his month on earth in the manner to which he'd become accustomed.

For some reason that notion didn't particularly appeal to him. Not that he thought there was a chance in hell, pardon the expression, to redeem himself, right the mysterious wrongs Augusta had insisted he'd committed, and make it past the Waystation. No, he was going to be roasting in the other place, there was no doubt about it, and he ought to be enjoying his brief sojourn on earth.

And he was. The room under the eaves at the Swensens was cold and barren, the bed narrow and saggy, the food plain and riddled with cholesterol. And yet he'd slept better in that narrow bed, beneath

Carrie Alexander's quilt, than he ever had in his life. The food tasted better, and he no longer had to worry about cholesterol, did he? Besides, butter and cream tasted so damned good.

But not as good as Carrie Alexander's mouth. He saw her sitting in the choir, dressed in a blue robe, her face serene and untroubled. Looking like a saint again, he thought gloomily. He shouldn't want to tarnish that sainthood. It wouldn't sit well with the powers that were overseeing him. It would send him to hell for sure, and they might not wait until Christmas Eve.

He should have asked more questions at the Way-station, he thought as he followed the train of Swensens down the center aisle to a spot near the front of the church. Near the choir. Would he be sentenced to the other place without hope of parole? Or did he get time off for good behavior? Credit for at least trying? Maybe it would behoove him to forget the potent effect Carrie had on him.

Damn it, he hadn't been that rotten in his previous life! It wasn't fair that he was sent back to make up for all the wrongs he'd committed. As far as he could remember he'd been no better or worse than the next man.

It wasn't going to be up to him. He sank into the pew next to little Harald, and a moment later Gertrude Hansen sat down beside him, her eyes unreadable behind the thick-lensed glasses.

"Good morning," he whispered, having ascertained that a certain amount of preservice talking was allowed in this church.

Obviously not by Gertrude. Her mouth thinned disapprovingly, and he wished he'd worn a tie. "Good morning," she replied. "What were you thinking about?"

Lustful thoughts of a choir member, he wanted to tell her. "I was admiring the simplicity of the church," he whispered back.

"Were you?" Gertrude's gaze must be sharp behind those thick glasses. She reached out and patted his hand with her own aged one. "We're glad you're here with us, Gabriel."

Not if you knew what I'd really been thinking, he thought, smiling faintly at her and turning his gaze back to the front of the church. And found himself gazing directly into Carrie's eyes.

If she remembered the circumstances when she'd last seen him, she'd appeared to put it out of her mind. Scratch that, of course she remembered. There was no doubt in his mind that she hadn't been kissed nearly enough. Even so, she'd obviously managed to wipe the memory from her mind, her gaze serene and impersonal, almost maternal.

Gertrude, sitting next to him, could be maternal. He wasn't about to accept that from the woman in the choir. He also wasn't about to send her lascivious messages from his seat in the congregation, not with Gertrude on one side and an impressionable Harald on the other. He simply stared at her for a moment, and his eyes said, "later."

She blinked, startled out of her serene state. Before she could react, the organ started, the congregation surged to its feet, and they were in the midst of "Wachet auf."

If he'd worried that she'd try to escape once the service was over he needn't have. The Scandinavian

population of Angel Falls wasn't about to let an oc-
casion go by without eating, and immediately after
church he was plied with coffee and a thin, wonderful
pastry called kringle as he was introduced to Larsens,
Swensens, Hansens, Johannsens, Rasmussens, and all
the "sens" that flesh is heir to.

He knew she was standing behind him before he saw
her. Even as he made strained conversation with the
gentle, slightly befuddled Pastor Krieger, he could feel
her presence, feel it through his clothes and skin like
a soft spring breeze. He'd never feel a spring breeze
again, he thought before turning, and a sudden wave
of sorrow hit him. He would have liked to have felt the
spring breeze against his skin. With Carrie beside him.

"You're very gifted," she said when he turned to
look at her.

She'd divested herself of her blue choir robe, and
she was wearing some sort of shapeless dress. He
found himself wondering exactly what kind of shape
she had under there, and then stopped himself. He was
still in church, even if the service was over. He could
at least make an effort at behaving himself. "I am?"
he said, resisting the urge to touch her mouth with his
fingers.

"The angels. I love them both. It's hard to believe
that someone as talented as Lars would show up. I've
decided you must be a gift from heaven."

He was getting used to it by this time, the odd, random statements that meant nothing to anyone but
him. He didn't even choke on the piece of pastry he'd
just swallowed. "How's your water doing?"

"Just fine. I didn't get a chance to thank you for your help on Friday night." She said it calmly, not avoiding his gaze.

Two could play at that game. "Anytime," he said.

He was rewarded with a faint color in her pale cheeks. "Who did you have in mind when you carved the second angel?" She quickly changed the subject. "He looks so familiar, and yet I can't quite place him."

A sudden uneasiness trickled down his spine. Both angels had looked familiar to him, and he'd had no idea where the vision had come from. Wherever it had sprung from, it had bypassed his conscious mind entirely. "I have no idea. I don't really think about what I do, I just do it." Truer than she realized, he thought.

"Of course I recognize Gertrude, and I think it's very clever of you to have seen through that myopic sweetness of hers. She loves to act charming and befuddled, but beneath those thick glasses she's really quite a formidable woman."

"What?" The sound of his shocked voice was enough to make several heads turn, and he immediately lowered his pitch. "What?" he demanded again.

"Gertrude. Your first angel is the spitting image of her, without her glasses, of course. Don't tell me you didn't realize it?"

"Where is she?" he demanded hoarsely.

"I think she got a ride back with the Milsoms. She left something behind for you with Lars."

"I imagine she did," he said, feeling oddly shaken.

"Were you still interested in doing some work for me?"

It took him a moment to regain his concentration. "What?"

"I asked if you were still interested in doing some carpentry work for me?" she repeated patiently, with still that faint trace of color in her cheeks.

He knew what she was doing. She was trying to prove to him, and to herself, that she was immune to his presence. That she could treat him with the same friendly distance she used for everyone.

"Do you think that's a wise idea?" he asked, more for her reaction than real hesitation. Wise or not, nothing was going to stop him from working on her ramshackle old house. Or on her.

"Why wouldn't it be?" She raised her chin defiantly.

"You tell me." He glanced over at the door. Lars was standing there, his brood surrounding him. "It looks like my ride's leaving. When do you want me out there?"

"Whenever's convenient for you. Tomorrow morning?"

"Assuming the Swensens will lend me a vehicle. Steve says my truck's going to be out of commission for a while."

Carrie made a face. "I don't think that will be a problem. If it is, I'll come and get you. I need to show you what needs work, and we can discuss how much I can afford to have done. And we need to make a few things clear."

He couldn't help it. He grinned, a slow, lazy grin that made the pale pink of her cheeks darken. "You mean like Friday night?" he murmured.

"Aren't you looking pretty?" One of the Hansens or Larsens came up and gave the flustered Carrie a big hug. "And aren't we lucky to have someone new in town? The way all the young people have been leaving, we've been afraid we'll turn into a ghost town."

"Why have all the young people been leaving?" Gabriel asked.

"When the mill closed down there was no work, outside the tourist trade," the elderly lady said. "I hear it's been happening all over the country, big corporations buy up little companies, and then they sell them off for a profit. It doesn't matter to some wheeler-dealer in New York that our lives are depending on them. It doesn't matter that's it's people they're dealing with. They just see it as numbers on a paper."

He wasn't enjoying this morning at all, he decided. There were only so many revelations he could handle at one time. Finding Augusta lurking behind a thick pair of glasses was bad enough. The fate of Angel Falls's mill was worse.

"What was the name of the factory?" he asked, not bothering to hide the strain in his voice.

For some reason Carrie was looking acutely miserable. "Precision Industries. Not a very distinctive name, was it? They made furniture, not very distinctive furniture, either, but good solid work."

He remembered Precision Industries, but just vaguely. There were so many companies along the way, bought up on a whim, disposed of just as lightly. He had made money on Precision's dissolution, but then, he always had made money. How much had it been—half a million dollars? Less? And where was it now? Beyond his reach.

"It happens," he said. "That's the way the system works."

"We don't think it works too well around here," the old lady said tartly, and he was reminded of Gertrude. And Augusta. "And considering the rest of the country, I wouldn't be too optimistic about how the system works."

There was nothing he could say to that. Fortunately he was spared trying to defend a system that had effectively destroyed the entire town of Angel Falls by the timely arrival of Lars.

"We're ready to go. Maggie's got some julekage rising and she needs to get back before it goes over the top. Why don't you get a ride back with Carrie?"

"No!" Carrie said with what he might have considered unflattering haste. Except that her nervousness around him was one of the deepest compliments he'd ever received. "I mean, I've got a million things to do," she floundered, looking miserable. Saint Carrie, who spent so much time trying to take care of others, was making a botch of it as for once she tried to protect herself.

"I'll come now," Gabriel said easily. "What time do you want me tomorrow?"

It was an innocent question, blandly stated. It shouldn't have caused that darkening in her eyes, the awareness she was fighting so hard. "Anytime in the later morning. Can he borrow a vehicle from you, Lars, or should I come get him?"

"Take the truck," Lars said with something dangerously close to a wink. "Take all the time you want."

Time was the one thing he didn't have. "Tomorrow morning," he said. A threat and a promise.

The aging American sedan that had held all six Swensens and his own lanky body was waiting out front. From a distance he could hear baby Carrie crying, Nils and Kirsten fighting, Harald whining, and Maggie's voice rising in the age-old sound of a mother driven to temporary distraction. He opened the front passenger door and took the baby from Maggie's arms without even considering what he was doing. In a moment the deafening howls had ceased to damp, shuddery sighs, and then she managed a small beatific smile up at him.

He stared down at the baby in his arms in utter astonishment. It had amazed him last night, when he'd had no choice but to take her, it amazed him this morning, when he'd willingly gone to her.

"You've got the touch, Gabe, my boy," Lars said cheerfully.

Gabriel met his gaze over the hood of the car. "You mean with children?" he asked, still dazed.

"Possibly. Definitely with women. Maybe just women named Carrie." He was grinning, obviously pleased with himself, and Gabriel wished he could respond. With a joke. With a moment of male camaraderie. But the fact remained that whatever had been born, was growing, between him and Carrie Alexander was doomed from the start. He needed to right the wrongs, save the souls he'd wounded. He couldn't leave Carrie in a worse place than the one where he'd found her three short days ago. Not if he wanted to end up in heaven.

So he said nothing, handing the now-cheerful baby back to her mother to strap into the car seat before cramming himself into the back seat with the three other Swensens.

"Gertrude left this for you," Harald said, handing him a heavy hardcover book.

"Thanks," Gabriel said absently, turning the book over with a sense of foreboding.

At least it wasn't Dante's *Inferno*. Not a religious tract, or a description of after-death experiences. It was something much more subtle, a message from Augusta, loud and clear. A novel, with the unsubtle title, *Fools Rush In*. And he remembered the rest of the quote. "Where angels fear to tread."

Was she calling him a coward or a fool? He really didn't give a damn. All he could think about was Carrie. At least for the time being. For now, the town of Angel Falls and the other lost souls could wait their turn.

CARRIE DROVE TOO FAST on the slush-covered roads, cursing herself all the way. Why in heaven's name had she been so foolish? She'd survive the winter if the house wasn't banked. She simply wouldn't leave on the very cold days, staying close to the fires to make sure they were putting out enough heat to keep the pipes from freezing. If they did freeze, she was capable enough to thaw them with the hair dryer.

She could take care of herself. She ought to eat more. Think about herself every now and then. When she'd come down with pneumonia last year, she'd ignored it until only Lars and Maggie's round-the-clock nursing kept her out of the hospital she couldn't afford. She mustn't let that happen again.

When it came right down to it, what was more important? Her uneasy awareness of Gabriel Falconi? Or the debt she owed the town of Angel Falls?

Never in her life had she been at the mercy of her libido. No, scratch that. Once, just once in her life had she made a complete fool of herself over a man. And it hadn't been as simple a matter as unexpected desire. She had loved Emerson MacVey. It had made no sense, but beneath those chilly blue eyes, that cool, heartless elegance she had glimpsed a lost soul.

She'd paid for her foolishness, paid in spades. She wouldn't make that mistake again. She could resist Gabriel, resist that faint trace of desire that flared up at unexpected moments.

"Liar," she said out loud, turning into her driveway. It wasn't a faint trace of desire. It wasn't an uneasy awareness. It was more powerful every time she saw him, fast becoming an obsession. That brief, tantalizing kiss had left her shaken, confused and longing for things she thought she'd given up and wouldn't even miss.

But she could fight it. She knew perfectly well he had the same sort of awareness of her, that kiss had been more than a hint. But they were in far different positions. He was self-reliant, a loner, on his way to a new life. She had the weight of the world on her shoulders. And there was no room in her life, even temporarily, for Gabriel Falconi.

She could do it. She was strong, determined. She could make things clear, in a calm, matter-of-fact way, that there could be nothing between them. And he'd accept it, turn his beautiful gaze toward someone else.

It was the least she could do. She needed help to make it through the winter, she had to face it. And she could either do what was painful, almost impossibly difficult, and have Gabriel Falconi around her house, working, and keep him at a distance. Or she could ask the Swensens, or someone else in Angel Falls, for help.

And she'd die before she'd do that. For one simple reason. The town was dying, turning into a ghost town because of the loss of the mill. Families were splitting apart, people moving away from a place where their grandparents had lived, and Lars Swensen was going to have to go into the woods and risk his life on a dangerous logging site.

No one would accept money from her if she offered them work. They foolishly thought she sacrificed too much for the people of the town as it was. Little did they know she had hardly begun. And that she owed so much more than she could ever repay.

There was one person to blame for all the catastrophes that had hit Angel Falls, and that was Caroline Alexander. If Gabriel Falconi was part of her penance, it was a small enough price to pay.

Chapter Eight

The tiny house was warm when Carrie walked in. She'd loaded the fires, tossed a few sticks of cinnamon into the bowl of water she kept on top of the stove, and the house smelled of Christmas. She hung her coat on the hook in the hallway and sank down at the kitchen table, folding her hands in front of her.

Something was nagging at the back of her mind, driving her crazy, and she couldn't figure out what it was. It was there, just out of reach of her conscious mind, and she wouldn't be able to concentrate on a thing until she remembered.

At least it had nothing to do with Gabriel Falconi, she knew that instinctively. It had been his presence that had sent the thought skittering away from her, and it would take her sternest self-discipline to call it back. Not to think about strong, work-worn hands, a tall, rangy body and the face of a fallen angel.

Angel, that was it! The angels that Gabriel had carved were beautiful and, oddly, eerily familiar. Lars had recognized Gertrude's expression in that stern old lady angel, as well, but none of them knew the golden-haired boy. No one in Angel Falls had ever seen the

man who bore an uncanny resemblance to that innocent angel.

Only Carrie, who'd looked at that youthful face and
seen the man she'd once been crazy enough to love.

Indeed, it should have come as no surprise to her
that she'd made a fool of herself over Emerson Wyatt
MacVey III. In truth, she'd been an accident waiting
to happen, an emotional bundle of female ready to fall
in love with the first unlikely prospect.

She couldn't dance. What had been astonishingly
gifted in Angel Falls, Minnesota, was stunningly mediocre in New York. Her gift was a dime a dozen, her
love of the dance worth nothing. She'd left the small
dance company where she'd finally managed to land
a job, left before they fired her. Accepting failure, accepting the loss of her lifelong dream with what she'd
foolishly assumed was a Scandinavian stoicism. Instead, she found she was simply numb.

The pursuit of that dream had taken most of her
life. She'd never had time for more than friendships in
her adolescent years, too caught up in pursuing her
dream of becoming a great dancer, somewhere along
the lines of Martha Graham crossed with Twyla
Tharp. If it hadn't been for a particularly determined
young man in college she would have reached the advanced age of twenty-three still a virgin. As it was, her
sexual experience was minimal and not all that exciting when she went to work for Emerson Wyatt
MacVey and found herself falling, illogically, head
over heels in love with him.

It wasn't as if there were much to recommend him,
apart from his rather conventional blond good looks.
The women she worked with despised him, he seemed

to have no friends, and his prevailing attitude was one of icy condescension toward all and sundry. He was utterly, completely alone.

It was that very aloneness that called to her. She thought she saw vulnerability beneath his remoteness, she thought she saw a wounded child who needed love and compassion. She thought she saw someone she could heal, and in doing so she would heal herself.

She'd been a fool, she knew that now. But back then, three seemingly endless years ago, he'd seemed to be everything she wanted. And the cooler, more foul tempered he was, the more she managed to convince herself that he needed her.

At first it had been subtle enough, her attraction to him. It might have stayed an unfocused maternal feeling if she hadn't seen him with his current girlfriend, seen the remoteness vanish into uncompromising sensuality, in the way he touched the striking young woman, in the way he looked at her. There was no warmth, but there was heat, and Carrie absorbed it, unobserved, shocked to find she wanted that heat directed at her.

She wanted him to notice her. She wanted to please him. In addition to that, she wanted to do something for her friends in Angel Falls, where the only viable industry, the mill, was running into deep trouble.

Emerson MacVey knew how to bring fresh life to failing businesses. He bought and sold them, invested in them, made them profitable. She'd thought if he directed even a fraction of his steel-trap mind toward Precision Industries of Angel Falls, Minnesota, then there would be no more layoffs, no more hard times.

She'd been subtle, knowing he wasn't a man who responded to pressure tactics, simply mentioning it in passing. The morning, early in December, when he'd stopped by her desk and asked her to get him all the information about Precision Industries had been a triumphant one. It was the beginning of the Christmas season, and she was going to secure for her hometown the greatest Christmas gift of all.

He wasn't a man who had affairs with his underlings. He wasn't a man who was prey to any weakness whatsoever. But the night of December twenty-third Carrie had come back to the office late, to pick up a present she'd left behind. MacVey was due at a fundraiser with his polished girlfriend, and the place would be deserted.

It wasn't. She used her key, letting herself into the tastefully decorated suite of offices, and began rummaging through her desk for the present she'd bought earlier that day, when she heard a sound from the inner office.

Music. Christmas music, but not the cheery kind. Something classical and Gregorian, more like a dirge than a carol. And she heard the clink of ice in a glass.

She stood motionless, feeling absurdly guilty. Wondering if he was alone behind that partially closed door. Wondering what he was doing.

Emerson Wyatt MacVey wouldn't be doing anything undignified, inappropriate or impulsive. She pushed the door open just slightly, thinking she'd ask if he needed anything.

He was sitting behind his glass-and-chrome desk, a bleak, cold expression on his handsome face. His blue eyes were distant, his Armani suit jacket had been discarded, his Egyptian-cotton shirt unbuttoned. She'd never seen him without a tie. With his blond hair ruffled. She'd never seen him with any emotion other than faint contempt.

"What the hell are you doing here?"

He never swore, either. His voice was rough, and she knew he'd been drinking. His eyes were red, but she didn't think that came from the amber-colored liquid in the glass beside his elegant hand.

"I left something."

"Go away."

She knew she should. MacVey was a private man—he wouldn't want her seeing him vulnerable. And vulnerable he was right now. Her heart cried out for him, and she stepped inside the room, closing the heavy door behind her. "Let me get you some coffee," she said gently.

He glared at her. "I don't need coffee. I've gone to a great deal of trouble to get drunk tonight, and I'm certainly not going to ruin the effect by drinking coffee. I'm not nearly drunk enough. You can go out and buy me more Scotch."

She shook her head, crossing the room to stand in front of the desk. "What happened?"

"'What happened?'" he mimicked, his voice savage. "Do you want to soothe my fevered brow, Carrie? Nothing happened, nothing whatsoever. It's Christmas, and I hate Christmas. The only suitable response was to get drunk."

"Where's Ms. Barrow?"

"Left me for another man."

"I see."

"No, you don't," he shot back. "You think I'm here drowning my sorrows because she left me. She was good in bed. Period. She was elegant to look at, and she didn't ask me stupid questions. But she wanted 'commitment.'" His voice was mocking. "She wanted 'intimacy.' She wanted me to bleed all over her, and I bleed for no woman."

"So why are you getting drunk?"

"A tribute to the season. Goodwill toward men, and all that crap."

She reached out for his half-filled glass of whisky, but his hand shot out and caught her wrist, stopping her. He hurt her, but she knew he didn't mean to. He just didn't realize how strong he was. They stayed that way for a moment, unmoving, as he sat there watching her, her wrist imprisoned in his hand.

And then his eyes narrowed, and a faint, mocking smile began to form on his thin mouth. And his thumb caressed her wrist. "You have a crush on me, don't you?"

Color flooded her face, and she tried to pull away. "Don't be ridiculous."

"I know the signs. It happens often enough, God knows why. It's usually the younger ones, who think I just need a good woman to make me happy. I don't need a good woman, Carrie."

"I'm sure you don't," she said stiffly. He released her finally, and she could still feel the warmth of his skin where he'd held her. "I'll be going now."

He rose, circling his desk, coming after her. Stalking her, though that notion was absurd in such a civilized man. "I just need a woman," he said, his voice low and cool and undeniably beguiling. "Do you want to be that woman, Carrie? Do you want to see whether you can save me?''

She'd reached the door, pulled it open, but his arm shot out and slammed it. She spun around, leaning up against it, staring at him. He wasn't much taller than she was, and in his cool, determined face she could still see the look of a lost child. One she wanted to comfort.

He stood there, his arms imprisoning her, his body not touching her. "It's up to you, Carrie," he said in a low voice. "Do you want me to let you go?"

He was warm. No, he was hot. He was staring at her out of pale, sensual eyes, and for the first time in her life she felt intense sexual attraction.

She would have denied it. She would have fought it, but her brain had melted, and somehow she thought that if she didn't take it, seize it, seize the moment, then the chance would never come again.

"No," she said, staring at him.

"No, what?"

"No, I don't want you to let me go."

He smiled then, a slow, cool smile that should have warned her. And then he set his mouth against hers, and no force in heaven or on earth could have stopped her.

He tasted of whisky. He tasted of coffee. He tasted of anger and despair. And all she wanted to taste was love.

She didn't want to remember that night, but there were times when it still haunted her, sleepless nights when she could feel his hands on her body.

He'd pulled her down onto the thick shag carpet and taken her fully dressed, only her serviceable cotton underwear flung away. He'd taken her on the leather sofa, naked, slippery, with the city lights all around them. He'd taken her leaning against the sink of his private washroom, he'd taken her in the marble shower stall. He'd taken her, had sex with her, shown her things she hadn't even imagined about her body that she thought she knew so well. The only thing he hadn't done was make love to her.

She had no illusions when she left just before dawn, left him sprawled and sleeping on the wide leather sofa, a cashmere blanket thrown over him. He hadn't allowed her to say a word of love, of affection, he hadn't allowed a caress from her. She was the recipient of his angry passion.

She was late to work the next morning. By the time she reached the office the other secretaries were bustling around importantly, and Megan greeted her with a grimace. "You had to pick today of all days to be late?" she questioned caustically.

Carrie wasn't about to give her the real reason. "It's Christmas Eve. No one does much business on Christmas Eve."

"You forget we're working for the Grinch. He was already at work when I arrived here this morning, and he's in the midst of dismantling one of his recent acquisitions. Nice job for the Christmas season."

Carrie had known. The sense of disaster had hung about her like a dark angel from the moment she'd left his arms that morning, and she'd tried to fight it off. "What do you mean?"

"You know as well as I do what he does," Megan snapped. "He buys up companies and guts them for parts, makes a huge profit, and leaves disaster in his wake. Lord knows why he picked on a small factory in Minnesota for destruction. There must be a profit in it somewhere.''

''Where in Minnesota?'' She barely recognized her voice.

''That's right, you come from around there, don't you?'' Megan popped a chocolate into her mouth, staring at her coolly. ''It's a place called Precision Industries in Angel Falls. He's sold the equipment to a company in Utah, he's closing the plant, and right now he's deciding between an offer from someone to dismantle the building for scrap or to just leave it a rusting hulk as a tax loss. Nice Christmas gift for that town.''

''I have to see him.''

''As a matter of fact—'' Megan sounded a little more human ''—I'm afraid he's got a little Christmas gift for you.'' She handed Carrie a long envelope.

Carrie just stared at it for a moment. She didn't want to take it, but the other two women in the office were watching her, as well, and the only thing she could salvage was her pride.

She took it with a brief, unconcerned smile. ''I need to talk to him.''

Megan shook her head. ''He said no. I've already cleared your desk for you. You'll find your severance package more than generous. You can continue with your medical coverage, and you've got severance pay...''

Carrie opened the envelope. The check was there, insultingly large. Along with a scrawled note. One word, written in his bold, slashing handwriting. ''Sorry.''

Carrie ripped the envelope in half and dropped it onto the floor. "I don't need any benefits," she said. "I just want to see him."

"He's authorized me to call security if you prove difficult."

Carrie just looked at her. Without a word, she turned and walked from the building, leaving the pathetic box of her belongings behind her, leaving her heart and her innocence behind her.

She hated him. She wanted to kill him, she who was the gentlest of creatures. He'd destroyed her, he'd destroyed her town, for nothing more than a whim and a profit. She had no illusions about why he'd fired her. She'd seen him at his most vulnerable last night. He wouldn't want a reminder of that.

And he wasn't even man enough to face her, to tell her himself. He let his secretary do the dirty work, and if she had any sense at all she'd hate him. And she would, as soon as she got over the shock, as soon as her mind settled, as soon as she realized . . .

She'd never seen the taxi. One moment she was struggling for her sanity, the next she was struggling for her life. By the time she was well enough to think about Emerson Wyatt MacVey, he was already dead of a heart attack. And all she could do was cry.

She hadn't wanted to think about him, Carrie thought, staring out into the snowy Minnesota countryside. She thought she'd been able to put him out of her mind, concentrating instead on somehow making things better for the poor beleaguered town she'd brought to destruction. Atonement, penance, all those nice, stern biblical phrases that had little to do with the innocent joy of Christmas.

But ever since Gabriel Falconi had shown up at her doorstep she'd been thinking about Emerson. Remembering.

She had no difficulty understanding why, whether she wanted to accept the truth or not. Gabriel and Emerson had absolutely nothing in common, apart from an odd kindred expression in the back of the eyes, one she couldn't even begin to define.

The only thing they shared was Carrie Alexander.

For the first time since Emerson MacVey she was attracted to someone. She didn't like it, didn't want to accept it, but denying it seemed impossible. She was attracted to Gabriel, with his deep, slow voice, his strong hands, his angelic beauty and his tall, graceful body. And it was only logical that her attraction would bring back memories of the last man she'd been fool enough to want.

She couldn't deny her attraction, but that didn't mean she had to give in to it. She'd done her best to make it clear to Gabriel that she wasn't in the market for a brief affair with an itinerant carpenter. She wasn't in the market for a long-term commitment with Prince Charming, for that matter. She wasn't going to think about her wants, her needs, her weaknesses. She had her penance, and nothing was going to get in the way of it.

She should eat something, she knew it. A lifetime of watching her weight had left her with little interest in food, but she knew she had to keep her strength up. She should open a can of soup, then start work on the Christmas quilt she was making for Mrs. Robbins.

It needed to be special. Mrs. Robbins had commissioned it as a Christmas present for her only granddaughter, the granddaughter she hadn't been able to buy a wedding present for. The amount Carrie was charging her wouldn't even cover the materials, but Mrs. Robbins didn't know that. It was just one small thing Carrie could do to try to make amends.

Mrs. Robbins was only one of the people whose lives had been torn apart by the closing of the mill. Her two sons had lost their jobs, and they'd already taken their families and relocated to Saint Cloud. The only family the elderly lady had living nearby was her newly married granddaughter, and she was there on borrowed time. If there were no jobs, they wouldn't be able to afford to stay, and Mrs. Robbins would be alone.

Fresh snow was falling, and a brisk north wind was whipping the flakes against the house. Carrie hoped it wouldn't be a windy winter. The old house was snug enough as long as the wind didn't blow. Once it did, not even the wood stove could make a dent in the chill that invaded the place.

Gabriel would come over tomorrow and fix up the banking around the foundation, repair some of the windows, make things snug and tight. In return she'd give him some of the money she had saved, the small amount she was parceling out to the needy. She didn't know why she thought Gabriel was needy. Maybe it was that look in his eyes, so different and yet oddly like Emerson's. And she'd never known a man more needy than Emerson Wyatt MacVey.

She had to stop thinking about him. Had to stop thinking about Gabriel Falconi, for that matter. She wasn't interested in sex—it only led to disaster. She wasn't interested in love, either. Falling in love with

Emerson MacVey had been the worst mistake of her life. She had trusted him, and he'd turned out to be a conscienceless snake. It didn't mean she no longer loved him. But she never should have put her town into his ruthless hands. Not to mention her heart.

It was past time for regrets. It was the first Sunday in Advent, Christmas was coming, and despite their depressed economy Angel Falls was going to have the best damned Christmas in memory. Carrie was determined.

GABRIEL STOOD in his tiny room at the Swensens', stooped under the eaves, looking out at the snow-covered town to the factory on the hill. As industrial buildings went, it wasn't a bad-looking building. If only it were someplace like Massachusetts it could have been turned into a trendy apartment building, or an upscale mall.

But the people of Angel Falls had no way to pay for trendy apartments or upscale malls. They could barely afford to live in this demanding climate, much less treat themselves to the luxuries that had once bored him.

And it was his fault. He no longer had any doubts about that—it had been MacVey's corporate greed that had gutted this economy, sending the town on a downhill slide just as the country was pulling itself out of its decline. He could no longer remember the details, or even why he'd done it. That life was becoming hazier and hazier, the man who'd done those deeds seemed only a distant kin to Gabriel Falconi.

But done it he had. And there was no doubt where his second miracle had to come from. He had to somehow make things right, if not for the whole damned town, at least for the Swensen family.

Three years ago it would have been simple. He had money and power to spare. Now he had a gold credit card, a few hundred dollars in cash, and a miracle per person, a power he needed to use wisely.

He glanced over at the book on his dresser. He never read novels, never had the time for them, and he doubted Gertrude/Augusta meant more than a jab at his temporary security. Still, the Swensens were busy with family activities, and he didn't want to intrude. His truck was still broken down, and the wind was howling outside, whipping the snow into a frenzy. He was in no mood to go for a walk.

Unless Carrie Alexander's house was within walking distance, and he knew full well it wasn't. He only had a few weeks here, and he didn't want to waste a moment of it.

But she'd looked frightened of him. He'd recognized that when she'd looked up at him, and he wondered what scared her. His kiss? Or something else?

What had MacVey done to her? For some reason his memory remained blank. He knew he'd fired her— Augusta had gleefully informed him of that. And that she'd been the only one to cry for him when he died.

Had she loved him? He knew he couldn't have slept with her—Emerson MacVey had been a conscienceless scum but he didn't sleep with his secretaries.

But there was something there. Something in that cockeyed triangle that existed uneasily between them. Between Carrie and Gabriel and his old self. And he wasn't going to get any further with rescuing Carrie until he found out what it was.

He turned away from the snowy landscape, from the brooding hulk of the old brick factory, and picked up the book. The room was chilly with the door closed, so he burrowed down under the quilt Carrie had made. It was soft, warm, and smelled like her perfume. If only she was there with him.

A stupid thought, one Augusta would probably hear from halfway across town and punish him for. This mission was doomed from the start—he might as well enjoy the small amount of time he'd been allotted and then take his punishment like a man.

Opening up the book, he began to read.

Chapter Nine

Oh, God, it smelled like cookies. Cinnamon and spice, ginger wafting through the small, decrepit farmhouse when Gabriel let himself in the next morning. Coffee, as well, with the tang of hazelnut to sweeten it. He wasn't sure how he knew it was hazelnut, but there was no doubt in his mind.

Cookies were laid out on sheets of wax paper all over the spotless kitchen. Some with red and green sprinkles, others pressed into ornate shapes. The coffee was on the stove in an old aluminum drip pot, and he could hear the steady splash as it brewed.

The place was bursting with warmth, but then, it was a moderate day outside. He was rapidly growing used to the chill temperatures of Minnesota, so that a sunny high of twenty degrees seemed positively balmy. He shrugged out of the ancient peacoat that seemed to be Gabriel Falconi's defense against the winter and hung it on the wooden peg near the door.

The old house was filled with comfortable sounds, as well as smells. The drip of the coffee, the crackle of the fire, the sound of the shower running. And Carrie's voice, loud and tuneful and surprisingly cheery, singing "God rest ye merry, gentlefolk."

Surely that was wrong? "Merry, gentlemen," wasn't it supposed to be? Lord help him, Carrie Alexander must be a closet feminist, as well as a saint set on self-destruction.

In the past there had been nothing that annoyed MacVey more than feminists. For some reason this morning Gabriel found himself smiling. God rest ye, merry gentlefolk, indeed. It sounded better that way.

Her wood box needed filling. Despite the fact that there was nothing he would have liked better than to sit at her table and drink coffee and eat cookies and wait to see whether she'd emerge from the shower fully dressed or not, the distant memory of Augusta's stern eyes squashed that temptation. It took him three trips to fill the wood box, and he deliberately made enough noise so she wouldn't make the mistake of emerging from the bathroom in a towel, but he still felt a shaft of disappointment when she greeted him at the door wearing a turtleneck tunic that reached from her chin to her knees.

He rose above his baser nature to realize it was a wonderful piece of clothing. Bright red and Christmassy, it was made of a soft cottony yarn, and it molded against her reed-slim dancer's body and moved with her grace.

And then he frowned. She was more than reed slim. She was downright skinny. "You're too thin," he said as he stomped the snow off his feet and kicked the door shut behind him, sounding more gruff than he'd meant to.

Carrie blinked in surprise, and then a slow, luscious smile curved her pale face. "Good morning to you, too," she said cheerfully. "Thanks for filling the wood box. Do you want some coffee?"

"Yes," he said, knowing he sounded grumpy. He moved past her into the living room, dumping the wood with a loud crash before turning to look at her. Her skin was flushed from her shower, and this morning she didn't look the slightest bit wary. She looked firm, decisive, in control. And he found himself wondering if he could make her lose her control.

She'd already moved back into the kitchen, pouring them both mugs of the fragrant coffee, and he told himself he was there to save her, not to sleep with her. He took one of the pressed-back chairs, spun it around and straddled it, accepting the coffee from her with a muttered thanks.

She took the chair farthest from him, a fact that pleased him. Obviously she wasn't as secure as she wanted him to believe. He liked that. "Have a cookie," he said, taking a sip of the coffee. It was good enough to die for.

Carrie shook her head. "I'm not hungry. You have some."

"You're never hungry. You don't eat enough to keep a bird alive."

"Birds eat three times their weight every day."

"You're awfully sassy for a woman who's starving to death."

"I'm not." The light still danced in her eyes, and she seemed to have forgotten she was going to be stern with him. She reached out and took a cookie, popping it into her mouth defiantly.

"Who are the cookies for?"

"What makes you think they're not for me?" she countered.

"Because as far as I can tell, you don't do a damned thing for yourself."

She ate another cookie. "I don't think that's any of your business."

Gabriel shrugged. "I suppose it isn't. I guess I'm just not used to being around saints."

"I'm hardly that." She took a third cookie without realizing it. It was a gingerbread man, and she bit off his head with her sharp white teeth. "As a matter of fact, I've spent too much of my life around people who were only out for their own good. Who squashed anyone or anything that got in their way."

She was talking about MacVey, he knew it. He took a meditative sip of his coffee. "Whoever he was, he obviously didn't appreciate you."

"What are you talking about?" She'd devoured cookie number three, and was on her way into number four, an ornate, pecan-studded horn.

"The man who squashed anyone or anything that got in his way. I take it you were one of the ones he squashed."

He wondered if he'd pushed her too far. He wanted to know what she really thought of Emerson MacVey. Did she still hate him? Did she have reason to? Damn it, if only he could remember!

She put the half-eaten cookie down. "If you're finished with your coffee I can show you what needs doing around here."

"Did you love him?"

He wasn't sure what he expected. Not the faint shadow of sorrow that danced in her blue eyes, not the wry, self-deprecatory smile that curved her mouth. "I did," she said, rising from the table with her dancer's grace. "Hearts are made to be broken, Gabriel. Trust is made to be betrayed. End of discussion." She started toward the door, but Gabriel forestalled her.

"Do you still love him?"

She turned to look up at him. It was still a strange feeling, looking down into her blue eyes. In the past, he hadn't been that much taller than she was.

In the past, he remembered with sudden, shocking clarity, he'd covered her body with his, and the fit had been perfect. She'd wrapped her legs around him, taken him inside her, and for one night and one night alone he'd lost himself and his miserable existence in the sweet pliant warmth of her body.

"He's dead," she said flatly. Her eyes narrowed. "Are you all right? You look as if you'd seen a ghost."

"I just remembered something," he muttered, still reeling from it.

"It mustn't have been anything pleasant."

"I wouldn't say that," he managed to drawl. "So your true love broke your heart, betrayed your trust and then died. It must give you comfort to think of him roasting in the flames of hell for what he did to you."

"I'm not into revenge, Gabriel," she said. "And besides, I don't believe in hell."

"Do you believe in heaven?"

"Yes."

"Then what's the good of heaven without hell?"

She smiled then, and her mood seemed to lighten. "When you find out, Gabriel, be sure to let me know."

It was moments like these, Gabriel thought, watching her step out into the bright winter sunshine, that scared the hell out of him.

She didn't know. She couldn't know. If he tried to tell her she wouldn't believe him. But the eerie appropriateness of her words haunted him as he followed her out into the day.

CARRIE BEGAN BOXING UP the cookies in the various tins she'd been collecting. The sound of a hammer echoed pleasantly beneath the sound of Christmas music on the old stereo, and she smiled to herself as she worked. Gabriel was outside, fixing the banking around the sagging foundation of the old farmhouse, and the steady sound of his work was as soothing as the smell of cinnamon and coffee. He'd looked faintly surprised when she'd shown him around the place, enumerating the things that needed to be done. She wasn't quite sure what he expected.

He might have thought she'd asked him out here for the sake of his beautiful face, but he would have been wrong. He must be used to women coming up with excuses to have him around. There simply weren't that many men who looked like that, with a quiet, non-threatening manner besides. Not that he was as quiet as he seemed. There was a sharp, mocking intelligence at war with the gentleness in his dark eyes. Whenever she looked at him, really looked, she had the odd notion she was looking into the eyes of two different people.

He was right about one thing, she hadn't manufactured the work she had him do. It was needed, but in other circumstances she would have let it wait.

But he was a stranger in town, stranded, with no work and no money. It was her fault the factory had closed down, her responsibility to help those affected by it. If Precision Industries were still a viable alternative, Gabriel could have worked there through the holiday season.

He wasn't a man who asked for help, a man who wanted to accept help. She could understand that—she felt the same way. There were a great many people in town whose pride got in the way of their need, and Carrie had grown adept at circumventing that pride.

Because there was a major difference between her and the people of Angel Falls. They didn't deserve their misfortune. She did.

She'd berated her ego time and time again. If only she hadn't thought she could save the world. Save the factory, save her beloved Angel Falls, save Emerson MacVey. Instead, her well-meaning actions had brought despair and disaster. And Emerson MacVey had doubtless forgotten her existence months before he died.

Why did she keep thinking about him? Ever since Thanksgiving he'd been haunting her dreams, her waking hours, as well. She'd thought she'd gotten past it all, down to the point where she only thought about him once or twice a week. But suddenly it was all fresh and new, the heat of her attraction to him, the pain of his betrayal, the shock and sorrow of his death. She'd come to terms with it all, knowing her energies needed to be channeled into making a difference, not bemoaning the past.

But he seemed to be hovering just beyond her consciousness, a ghost, a spirit, a longing that she hadn't quite recovered from. She wondered if she ever would.

She wrapped a bright velvet ribbon around the last tin and sighed. They were a small enough offering, but they were something, and she had her deliveries to make that afternoon, once she was certain Gabriel had enough to do. She sank down at the round table, muttering a tired "damn." She'd forgotten to eat yesterday, and sugar cookies for breakfast along with black coffee weren't the most nutritious choice.

She leaned her head back, but the room began to swirl around her. She needed to get up and put wood on the stove, she needed to get up and answer the telephone that had just started ringing. She tried to rise, but the swirling surrounded her once more, and she felt herself start to fall into the blackness. She put out a hand to save herself, but there was no one there, she was alone, in the darkness, and she was falling, falling...

He caught her. Warm strong hands reached for her, pulled her back from that abyss, held her against a hard, muscled body. She could hear his voice, almost from a distance, cursing, she could feel the panicked beat of his heart as he lifted her in his arms. She wanted to say something, to tell him not to make such a fuss, but for some reason the words weren't coming, and she had to close her eyes, to lean her head against his shoulder.

Lord, he had nice shoulders, she thought dizzily. Strong, slightly bony, but so comfortable beneath the faded flannel shirt. She wanted to bury her face against that soft flannel. He smelled of wood smoke and fresh lumber and hazelnut coffee, and she wondered what his mouth would taste like. If she only moved her head a fraction of an inch she would find out.

He set her down on the sofa, and she clung to him for a moment, unwilling to let him go. He was warmth, safety, he was someone she didn't need to take care of. He was someone who would scare away the demons and keep her safe, and she was so tired of fighting.

And then she released him, sinking back against the sofa, her eyes closed. "Sorry," she murmured faintly.

"What happened?"

His voice was rough with concern, and his hands were in her hair, pushing the strands away from her face. She didn't want to open her eyes. If she did, she'd find him staring down at her, and she wasn't sure if she could keep the longing from her own eyes.

"You're right," she said. "I don't eat enough. Too much sugar and caffeine on an empty stomach."

"Damn," he said.

She opened her eyes at that, managed a weak smile. "Don't worry, it's happened before. I'll just make myself a cup of tea and some toast and I'll be fine…"

"You'll stay right there," he said fiercely.

His beautiful face looked enchantingly stern. "Listen, I'm okay," she said, trying to sit up, but Gabriel put one of his large, beautiful hands smack in the middle of her chest and pushed her back down again.

"Stay put," he said, "or I'll sit on you. I'm making you soup, hot milk, toast, and anything else I can find."

His words sent sudden panic through her. "I'm not hungry. Gabriel..."

But he was already rummaging around in the kitchen. She struggled to sit up, but the room whirled around her, and eventually she gave up. She just needed a moment or two to compose herself, and then she'd explain to him...

"You have no food in this house."

He was back too soon, and she wasn't quite up to arguing with him. "Of course I do," she said weakly. "There are at least ten dozen cookies..."

"You have a little bit of sugar and flour left over, and that's that. No milk, no bread, a couple of tea bags, a can of tomato paste, and a can of okra, for heaven's sake. Why in the world would you have a can of okra sitting on your shelves?"

"It was the only thing I couldn't bring myself to eat," she said, unable to resist. "I just haven't had a chance to get to the store recently. I was planning to go out this afternoon after I got you started. I'm going to deliver the cookies and then stop by the store and stock up on my way home."

"You're not driving anywhere."

"I beg your pardon?"

"If you want to go to the store I'll drive you. If you passed out behind the wheel and killed someone I'd never forgive myself." He looked half-surprised at his own words, but nevertheless completely stubborn.

"I'm not going to endanger anyone else," she said quietly.

"When you don't take proper care of yourself you endanger everyone else's peace of mind. Consider that the next time you forget to eat."

She couldn't argue with him. It was an unpalatable truth. Whether she deserved it or not, the people of Angel Falls cared about her. And the odd thing was, she knew they'd love her even when they knew the truth about what had happened to the factory. That it hadn't been some random choice of a power-mad conglomerate. That in her misguided efforts to play God she'd brought about its destruction.

"You can drive me to the store," she said wearily, the fight suddenly leaving her. "But you'll still be getting paid."

"You don't have anything better to do with your money in a town like this?" he countered. "I have to go to the store, too."

She sat up, and the whirling had blessedly stopped, at least for now. "You know, Gabriel, you have the most annoying habit of being right?" she said.

"I do my humble best. You feel up to going now?"

What she wanted to do was crawl under the covers and go to sleep. She was so tired, not even the rest of the pot of coffee could put energy into her. But Gabriel wasn't going to let her hide. Taking him on as another one of her pet projects might prove to be a costly mistake in a life strewn with mistakes.

"Now's as good a time as any," she said brightly, doubting she'd fooled him even for a moment. Those oddly familiar brown eyes could see her far too clearly.

An hour later she knew she should have been firm. They'd dropped the cookies off at the church, where the Ladies' Fellowship would distribute them, and then headed on to Martinsen's supermarket. Everyone had watched as they traversed the aisles, benign expressions on their faces, and she knew just what they were thinking. And the fact that in another lifetime, she would have wanted it to be true, only made it worse.

To top things off, Gabriel kept throwing things into her grocery cart. A dozen cans of chicken-rice soup, at eighty cents a can. Fruit juice, the expensive kind, imported crackers, yogurt, pasta, garlic, onions...

"What are you doing?" she demanded as he tossed a package of frozen bread sticks into the overflowing basket. "This is too much food for one person."

"Most of it'll keep. And I'm making you dinner tonight."

"Gabriel..."

"Carrie..." he mimicked right back, looking down at her and smiling.

For a moment she couldn't breathe. For a moment all memory of Emerson MacVey and the lifetime of stupid mistakes vanished, as she looked up into the warm brown eyes of Gabriel Falconi and fell in love.

The noise of the store was all around her. Old Mrs. Johannsen was moving past her, heading for the taco chips, Mr. Draper was over by the magazine rack, staring longingly at the computer magazines, and Jeffie Baker was standing near the wine rack looking furtive. Carrie was aware of all of them, but for a moment all she could concentrate on was the man in front of her, so close she could feel his body heat, so close all she had to do was sway against him and his strong arms would come around her and hold her tight and safe.

And then reality intruded. She pulled herself away, turning to watch Jeffie tuck a bottle of wine beneath his bulky down parka.

She didn't think she'd said a word, just made a quiet little sound of distress. No one else noticed what had happened. No one but Gabriel.

He moved with a speed and grace surprising in such a big man. With seeming clumsiness he bumped into Jeffie, knocking him against a small display of wine. The bottle he'd stolen fell with a thump onto the carpeted floor, along with half-a-dozen others.

"God, I'm clumsy," said Gabriel, who had to be the least awkward man Carrie had ever seen. He set the wine bottle back up on the stand, taking the one Jeffie had tried to steal and putting it back where it belonged on the shelf. The small crowd involved in midday shopping quickly returned to their own interests, and the conversation between Jeffie and Gabriel was low pitched enough not to reach her ears.

It looked pleasant enough, if earnest. Jeffie obviously thought Gabriel was God. She only hoped Gabriel had the sense not to humiliate him. It was hard enough to be seventeen, and even harder if you were blessed with such mindlessly intellectual twits as Jeffie had for parents.

She made a furtive trip down the aisles, hoping she'd be able to put a few things back, but Gabriel caught up with her just as she was reshelving the horridly expensive chicken soup, and he took the can out of her hand. "I gave him hell," he said pleasantly.

She was shocked. "You didn't! He's sensitive, Gabriel, you might make things worse. . . ."

"For some reason he takes it from me. Maybe he's just grateful for the attention. He needs someone to knock some sense into him. If my father had caught me doing something like that I wouldn't have sat down for a week."

"But Jeffie's father doesn't even notice."

"I know what that's like, too."

"Make up your mind, Gabriel. Either your father ignored you or he taught you right from wrong. Which is it?"

"I have a vivid imagination. Let's get out of here." He reached over and took two more cans of chicken soup and threw them into the cart.

She didn't have enough money to pay for all the things he'd taken from the shelves. Not and pay him, too, and give Pastor Krieger the money she'd promised for the Christmas fund. People needed that money, to buy food, to buy fuel, far more than she did.

She stared up at him in mute distress, unwilling to tell him the truth. She'd forgotten how astute he was behind those warm brown eyes.

"Why don't you go out to the car and wait for me?" he suggested calmly.

"I have to pay for the groceries."

"No, you don't."

"Yes, I do," she said furiously. "I don't take charity..."

"I know, you give it. Too damned bad, Saint Carrie. I chose this food, I'm paying for it, and I have every intention of eating a good portion of it. If you want to have a screaming row in the middle of the local grocery store I'd be more than happy to give it to you."

"I don't have screaming rows," she said between clenched teeth.

"Maybe you should. It would be good for you."

She stared up at him. The damnable thing about him was he was right. He was bringing up emotions, feelings she thought she'd managed to squash in her effort to atone for her sins. In the week since he'd arrived in Angel Falls she'd experienced lust, love, longing and sheer fury, when all she was used to feeling was quiet regret. It was oddly unnerving.

"I'll write you a check," she said tightly, enjoying the race of blood in her veins, enjoying her temper.

"You do that. When I'm finished my work, you can add it in. After Christmas, when I'm ready to leave."

"I don't have that much work to keep you busy," she protested.

"I take my time. Pay me after Christmas."

She wanted to hit him. She who never had hit anyone in her entire life. She whirled around and stalked toward the door, her dignity around her like a cloak. Mrs. Johannsen's knowing smile only irked her more.

He was out in five minutes, with four overflowing bags of groceries. He was humming under his breath as he stowed them in the back of her car, something familiar yet oddly jaunty. She recognized it with a start of shock. It was an up-tempo version of the Gregorian dirge that passed for Emerson MacVey's taste in Christmas music.

"How did you manage to pay for all that?" she demanded grumpily. "I thought you didn't have much money."

"Yeah, but I have a gold credit card," he said, sliding behind the driver's seat.

"Credit cards have to be paid off sooner or later."

For a moment he looked abashed. Then he started the car. "Don't worry," he drawled. "My credit card's got a rock-solid guarantee."

"Fasten your seat belt."

"You *are* in a grumpy mood, aren't you?" he said cheerfully. "I don't believe in them."

"In my car you wear seat belts," she snapped.

"Yes, ma'am." He seemed almost pleased by her bad temper. "But trust me, it won't matter."

"It can be the difference between life and death."

"Not in my case."

He drove well. Not too fast, his big hands resting on her steering wheel. She tried not to watch him, tried to concentrate on the melting slush on the back roads. Her temper was fading, guilt was setting in. He was only trying to help her, and she was an ungrateful, self-centered bitch to fight him.

"I'm sorry."

"I knew that would happen. Don't be sorry, Carrie. Be mad. I'm high-handed, and you like to be Lady Bountiful. It drives you crazy to have to accept anything in return. Admit it."

"I'm trying to be gracious," she said sharply.

"I like you better when you're honest."

"I don't give a damn what you like."

He turned and smiled at her, that wide, beautiful smile that would have melted the resolve of a saint. "Yes, you do," he murmured, then turned his attention back to the road, humming once more.

"Aren't you driving a little too fast?" she roused herself long enough to ask. The road was wide and blessedly deserted, but her car seemed to be picking up speed as they started down a long winding hill. "This isn't the Indianapolis 500, you know."

"I know." There was a certain tension in his voice, and the hands on the steering wheel were no longer gripping it loosely.

"Then why are you driving so fast?"

He didn't turn to look at her. His face looked grim in the winter light. "Because, Saint Carrie," he said with deceptive calm, "you don't seem to have any brakes."

Chapter Ten

He was a hell of a good driver. He realized that later on, but for the moment he'd been too intent on keeping Carrie alive to even think about it. Just as well. Emerson MacVey had been a clumsy, careless driver, treating his Mercedes with a singular lack of respect. If Gabriel had taken the time to consider it they might have ended up wrapped around a tree.

Carrie hadn't said a word as he wrestled with the speeding momentum of the car as it careened toward the bottom of the last hill before her old farmhouse, and he hadn't taken the time to do more than glance at her. Her face was pale, her hands were tightly clasped, but she looked serene, damn it. As if she were waiting for death.

The thought infuriated him enough to make him stomp on the gas just as they slid into a curve. It provided enough momentum to avoid a lethal clump of trees, but then the car went spinning, spinning, across the ice-covered road, finally coming to a shuddering halt. They sat in complete silence for a moment, and then he turned to look at her.

"Are you okay?" His voice was harsh, angry, and he didn't bother to disguise it.

She reached down for her seat belt, and he noticed with fury that her hands weren't even shaking. "Fine. You're a very good driver."

"Don't you even care?" he exploded.

She stared at him in blank surprise. "About what?"

"You could have died. It was a damned close call—we were headed straight for that clump of trees."

"But we didn't," she pointed out with maddening calm.

"But we might have."

She climbed out of the car. "The house is just over the next rise. We might as well start walking."

He tried to follow her, forgetting that he'd put his seat belt on. His own hands were shaking, a fact that infuriated him even further, and then he was following her as she trudged determinedly up the snowy hill.

He didn't say another word as they made their way the quarter mile or so to the house. He didn't worry about her getting too cold in the threadbare coat she was wearing—he was so damned mad it was lucky the entire state of Minnesota didn't melt under the heat of his fury. He followed her into the kitchen, slammed the door behind him, and caught her by the arm as she was starting to pull off her snow-covered coat.

"Do you have a death wish?" he demanded harshly.

She held very still, looking up at him. The snow had melted in her silky blond hair, dampened her long eyelashes, and he couldn't mistake the heated flicker of sexual awareness before she did her best to tamp it down, to give him that maternal, wise look that only increased his fury.

"I'm pragmatic enough to know that when it's my time, there's not much I can do about it. I'm not afraid of death."

"No," he said. "You're afraid of life."

Her face whitened, and she yanked at her arm, trying to free herself. He had no intention of letting her go. "What I'm afraid of is none of your business."

"You're afraid of life, of getting hurt, of making mistakes. You set yourself up as the saint of Angel Falls, ministering to the poor, soothing the weary, healing the sick. Too bad the lake's frozen over or you could show me how you walk on water."

She yanked again, and it only brought her up closer against his body. She was hot, he was hot, and he wondered that the kitchen didn't ignite. "Maybe I have a reason," she said furiously. "Maybe I need to make up to these people for the harm I've done them. Maybe I need to atone..."

"Atone for what? I can't imagine anything you might have done that would be so terrible."

"Then you haven't got a very good imagination."

He stared down at her for a long meditative moment. Her lips were soft, trembling now from anger and emotion, whereas her brush with death had left her unmoved. "I wouldn't say that," he murmured. "When I look at you I can imagine all sorts of things."

For the third time she tried to pull away. She backed up against the basement door, but he was with her, his body pressed up against her, and he wanted to see if he remembered the taste of her mouth, the feel of her body. He wanted to taste the life she was so blasé about losing.

He expected more resistance from her. He put his hand beneath her chin, tilting her face up, and took her mouth with a deep, searing kiss. Her hands were on his shoulders, but instead of pushing him away she was clinging to him. Her lips parted beneath his and she let him kiss her.

He tore his mouth away and stared down at her. "More charity, Carrie?" he said. "How far does your saintliness extend? Passive kisses? Or are you willing to take off your clothes and lie down for the poor itinerant stranger in need of comfort?"

He'd managed to reach behind that calm maternal facade, and her fingers dug into his shoulders as she tried to push him away. "You're disgusting," she said.

"No, I'm not. I'm human. At least for now. And I want you more than I've ever wanted anyone in my life. But I don't want a passive saint sacrificing her virtue. I want someone who wants me in return. I want a woman, not a martyr."

"Damn you," she began furiously.

"That's better," he murmured, and kissed her again.

This time there was no passivity about her. There was fury, passion, everything he'd ever wanted from her. She slid her arms around his neck, slanted her mouth beneath his, and kissed him back.

She was awkward, endearingly, erotically awkward at it, as if she hadn't been kissed enough lately. He remembered that about her. He cupped her face, his long fingers soothing her hair back away from her cheeks, and gentled the kiss, coaxing her, and the soft moan from the back of her throat rewarded him. He could feel her small breasts against his chest. Even through the thick layers of flannel he could feel her nipples harden in undeniable response, and he pulled her more tightly against him, wanting to drown in the physical sensations that were his only for a few short weeks. The heat, the touch, the sounds whirled around in his head, and he knew if he didn't stop there'd be no chance of saving her, or anyone else. Least of all, the very least of all, his own worthless soul.

He didn't pull away from her. He stroked her gently, softening the kiss, moving his mouth to her delicate ear, feeling her shudder in response. He tasted the delicate texture of her skin, breathed in her scent and told himself he had to stop. He held her, his head resting on hers, and waited for her breathing to slow, waited for his own heartbeat to steady, reveling in the fact that he had a heartbeat at all.

When the moment, the fever, seemed to have passed, he pulled away gently and looked down at her. She had a dazed expression in her wonderful blue eyes, and her mouth was soft and damp, and he would have given ten years of his life to kiss her again. But he had no years to give, so he released her, stepping back.

"Sorry," he said. "I shouldn't have done that."

"Why not?" Her voice was so quiet he could hardly hear her words, but he knew them in his soul.

"Because you didn't want it."

She looked up at him, her vision clearing. "Yes, I did." She moved across the room, heading for the telephone. "I'd better call Steve and see what he can do about the car."

She'd ended the subject, which was just as well. If they'd continued it he would have touched her again, and if he had touched her again, he wouldn't have been able to let her go.

The whole thing was damnable, he thought, watching as she spoke into the telephone, running a hand through her sheaf of silvery blond hair. At least this time her hands were shaking. A near brush with death had left her calm and unmoved. A brush with passion, with life, had shaken her to her roots.

"He'll be out as soon as he can," she said, hanging up the phone.

"Why do you need to atone?" he asked abruptly.

"I beg your pardon?"

"You said you had crimes you needed to atone for. Sins committed against this town that you needed to make up for. What were they?"

"None of your business." She put the kettle on the stove, busying herself, refusing to meet his eyes.

"You're right. But I don't pay proper attention to what is and isn't my business, and I fully intend to hound you until you confess your terrible sins. I imagine once you speak them out loud you'll find they aren't nearly so bad as you imagine."

She leaned back against the counter, staring at him. "This is a small town, Gabriel," she said flatly. "The people here relied on two things to survive. The tourist industry, which doesn't account for more than a few dozen families who spend the summer by the lake in makeshift cabins. And the factory. Precision Industries wasn't anything special, the work wasn't state-of-the-art woodcraft, but it provided a living for most of the people in town. With the factory closed down, no one has the money for houses, for food, for medicines, for gasoline. You've heard of infrastructures? Ours collapsed when the factory did."

"And where is your blame in all this? Did you fire-bomb the mill?"

She shook her head, refusing to meet his eyes. "You've already accused me of thinking I'm a saint. God-like delusions is a little more accurate. I thought I could save the mill, and instead I brought about its ruin."

He didn't want to hear this after all. He knew what was coming, knew with an instinct that transcended common sense, and he wondered if he walked out of the kitchen, climbed into Lars Swensen's beat-up old truck and just kept driving, whether he might live out his remaining three weeks in sybaritic pleasure.

Emerson MacVey would have done just that. But he was finding that he wasn't MacVey any longer. Neither was he Gabriel Falconi. He was some odd, uncomfortable mix of the two.

So he waited. Calmly, implacably, knowing she'd have to tell him. Which she did, her back to him as she stared out into the wintry landscape.

"I used to be a dancer, you know," she said in a dreamy voice. "Not a very good one, unfortunately. How was I to know that the best dancer Angel Falls, Minnesota, had ever seen was no more than adequate in New York City? I couldn't find work, but that wasn't the worst of it. The worst was knowing and accepting the fact that I was mediocre." She glanced over her shoulder at him, and there was a rueful, accepting expression on her face.

"So I took a clerical job in an office. Unfortunately I wasn't very good at that, either. I'd spent so much of my lifetime concentrating on being a dancer that I hadn't applied myself to much else. I managed to get a job working for a private investor in New York. A cold, ruthless bastard, if I do say so. And I made the dire mistake of falling in love with him.''

It was like a knife in his heart. It hurt more than the heart attack that had taken his life, it twisted inside him so that he wanted to scream in pain. In reality, he couldn't make a sound.

''Emerson made his money investing in small companies. Time after time he'd buy them and appear to bring them back to financial health, making a tidy profit as he did so. The problem was, I didn't realize how he did it. He cannibalized everything he could, selling off equipment, selling off smaller parts of larger conglomerates. He was utterly ruthless, and I'd fooled myself into thinking he was caring.''

''How could you have done that?'' Gabriel managed to say, amazed that his voice sounded no more than casually interested in the story she was telling.

''I thought he was a wounded soul, a good man hidden beneath his unfeeling manner. I thought he needed a good woman's love, I thought he would do the right thing when he was presented with the option.''

''And did you? Present him with the option?''

She tried to smile once more, but her expression was bleak. ''I told him about Precision Industries. Showed him what an excellent investment opportunity it was, for a man of his organizational skills. Unfortunately, he found it an even better investment opportunity as a tax loss. He sold off the equipment, fired all the workers, and sold the empty factory to the town for one dollar.''

"Then the town could sell the place..."

"It's falling into ruin. They've tried. No one's even remotely interested.''

"Did you tell him what you thought of him for doing that? Maybe he would have listened if you'd explained to him..."

"I doubt it. You see, he'd already committed the cardinal sin of having sex with me one night, and after that he wasn't ready to even see my face, much less hold a discussion.''

"If the two of you made love..."

"We didn't make love. He had sex with me. I made love with him. A subtle difference, I grant you, but enough to matter. He fired me the next day, rather than have to see me.''

"Carrie," he said, ready to tell her. Ready to confess his own sins, promise to make things better, to tell her he had cared about her, only he'd been cold and angry and frightened of needing anyone. "Carrie," he said, but the words refused to come.

Augusta had warned him. He could perform miracles, three of them, he could right the wrongs he'd done. But he couldn't tell anyone the truth about why he was here. Even when Carrie needed to hear.

She turned to look at him, and she managed a wry smile. "You're right," she said. "Confession is good for the soul.''

"You weren't to blame," he said, wondering how much he'd be allowed to say. "That bastard was.''

"Well, he's paid for his sins. He's dead, and has been for almost two years. I have to make up to Angel Falls for the harm I did."

"The harm *he* did."

She shrugged. "Nevertheless. There's nothing that can be done."

"You could sue his estate. He must have left a bundle..."

"No."

He didn't want to ask. He thought he'd heard more than he could bear; for some reason this would be the worst of all. He tried to move toward the door, but his feet were rooted to the floor. "You couldn't force yourself to bring suit..." he suggested in a hoarse voice.

She shook her head. "For this town, I would have done anything. After all, Emerson MacVey was beyond hurting. But his estate was worthless."

"Worthless?" he choked.

"Everything was delicately balanced. With his death, it all collapsed, like a house of cards. There was barely enough for a decent burial."

"How do you know?"

"I used to work for him, remember? One of my coworkers called and told me about it. She was very bitter. She said she'd put up with the arrogant bastard for eight years only to have him keel over and die on her, leaving her with absolutely nothing."

Megan, Gabriel thought, with one of those unexpected flashes of memory. "So it's up to you to rescue the town that he destroyed?"

She shook her head. "I don't think I'm God anymore. It's up to me to make things better, when and where I can. It's that simple."

"Punishing yourself while you do it."

"I'm not punishing myself."

He didn't want to argue with her anymore. She'd told him more things than he was ready to hear. He felt like Scrooge in *A Christmas Carol,* watching the hags argue over his bedclothes after he was dead. He'd died penniless. A worthy end for someone who had only cared about money and power.

"I'll go back and get the food out of the car," he said. "It's getting colder, and we don't want things freezing."

"You don't need to...."

"I do," he said irritably. "You curl up on the sofa with a cup of tea and I'll be back in a few minutes."

She glanced out the window. "It's snowing."

"It's always snowing. Go sit."

SHE WAITED UNTIL she saw him trudge down the driveway through the blowing snow, and then she let out a deep breath, one she hadn't realized she'd been holding. Her eyes were stinging, her heart ached, and she told herself she was coming down with the flu. And she told herself that Gabriel Falconi had far too unsettling an effect on her.

The kettle shrieked, just as she was about to succumb to an absolute orgy of self-pity. She stiffened her shoulders, made herself a cup of orange-spice tea, stirred in more honey than she usually allowed herself and went to curl up on the lumpy sofa in the living room.

He'd done a good job with the wood stove—the heat was still filling the room, but she pulled the quilt around her anyway, for protection as much as warmth. She needed something to hug around her, something to keep her safe.

She was going to send Gabriel Falconi away. Surely Lars could find work for him, or Steve. She couldn't have him in her house. looking at her out of those dark, haunted eyes. She couldn't let him put those elegant, beautiful hands on her, kiss her with that wide, hard mouth. She couldn't let herself be folded in his arms so that she could feel his heart beat, feel his need, a need that matched her own.

She'd loved one man in her life, in a moment of rash stupidity that had ruined not only her own future but that of an entire town. Now she stood on the edge of falling in love again, with a man who would leave in the new year, and for some reason it still felt like the same man. Gabriel Falconi and Emerson MacVey couldn't have been more different. One a glorious Renaissance angel, the other an overbred yuppie. One tall and strong and graceful, the other spare and slender and precise. One the child of immigrants, the other the child of privilege. One who worked with his hands and body, the other who'd never done a day's honest labor in his life.

So different and yet the same. The same lost soul, hidden behind disparate eyes. The same longing calling out to her, a longing that resonated in her heart.

A longing she had every intention of denying. She took a sip of the scalding tea, listening to the wind howl around her tiny house, rattling the windows that needed fresh caulk, knocking against the foundations that still needed banking. She'd have to do it herself.

She heard him come back, stomping into the kitchen, dumping the bags of groceries on her round oak table. She knew she should get up and help him, get up and confront him, but for the time being she stayed where she was, too weary, too comfortable to move.

She must have drifted off. She heard Steve's voice in the kitchen, making disparaging noises about her beloved station wagon. "Second accident in less than a week, Gabriel," he drawled. "You got a death wish or something?"

"Not particularly," he replied. "Her brakes failed. Think you can fix them?"

"Shouldn't be a problem. I'll tow it into town and get right on it. You're not in any hurry for your truck, are you?"

There was a pause, and Carrie found she had enough energy to wonder how he'd respond to that. He wanted to leave, she knew with sudden certainty. He wanted to get out of Angel Falls as much as she wanted him to go. "No hurry," he said finally, his voice resigned.

She should get up and tell Steve her car could wait. After all, Gabriel had bought her enough food to feed the Russian army—she'd have no need to go into town for days.

But she couldn't. She could barely keep her eyes open. She knew when Steve left, knew when Gabriel came back into the room. She wasn't asleep, but she had every intention of pretending to be.

He loaded the wood stove then closed it down again, before coming to stand over her. She didn't want to open her eyes, but suddenly she couldn't resist. She wanted to read the expression on his face.

It was a waste of time. He was more than adept at shielding his emotions, one small thing he had in common with Emerson MacVey. "You need to eat," he said gruffly.

"I will."

"I need to get back to town."

"I know."

He didn't move. He wanted to touch her, she knew it. She wanted him to touch her, as well. But he wasn't going to. "I've got a few things to do," he said. "I don't think I'll be able to come out for a few days."

Despair and relief flooded her. "That would be fine. I'm going to be rather busy myself the next few days. I'm not sure the work can't wait until next spring, if it comes to that."

He knew the nature of the work as well as she did, knew that it couldn't wait. "That might be a good idea," he agreed, moving away from her. "Take care of yourself."

He was saying goodbye. She knew it with a certainty that held no logic, and she felt a tearing of grief inside her. But she couldn't stop him. Couldn't put out her hand to reach him, to make him stay.

And then he was gone. She heard the sound of Lars's old truck as he drove away, and then nothing but silence, broken by the sound of the snow beating against the old windows of her grandmother's house, the dry crackle of the aged wood in the old stove.

She'd promised him she'd eat. She pulled herself off the sofa and wandered into the kitchen, trailing the quilt after her. He'd put all the food away, the first neat man she'd ever met in her lifetime. No, the second. Emerson MacVey had been a neat man, as well. She'd considered it a character flaw.

She didn't have the energy to heat herself some soup, so she made do with a carton of raspberry yogurt, leaning against the refrigerator door as she forced herself to swallow the stuff. Everything was tasting strange nowadays, which was just as well. It meant she had less interest in food and, therefore, could spend what little money she had on more important things.

She was so tired. She used her last bit of energy calling the Swensens' house. Maggie answered, sounded worried, and Carrie remembered belatedly that Lars was in the woods that day, working with Hunsicker's shoddy operation. She wished she could offer words of comfort, but at that moment she needed all her comfort for herself.

"Keep Gabriel from coming out here for a while," she managed to say.

"But why..."

"Trust me, Maggie. It's for the best." She was counting on Maggie's loyalty. Maggie would do anything for her, with many questions asked, of course, but she also accepted a total lack of answers. As she would today.

"Lars has a project he's working on in the evening. Maybe Gabriel will help."

"That would be wonderful," Carrie said wearily.

"Are you all right? You don't sound well."

"Just tired, Maggie. A few days' rest is all I need. I'll see you in church on Sunday."

"Carrie, are you certain...?"

"Wouldn't I tell you if I needed help?" It took all of Carrie's waning energy to sound practical.

"No."

"Keep him busy, Maggie," she said wearily. "I'll be fine."

She didn't convince Maggie, and she didn't convince herself. She just needed some rest. She wandered back into the living room, sinking down on the sofa. It was too hot in the room, and yet cold, as well, and she huddled deeper into the quilt, looking for something that had already driven away from her, back to the Swensens' house in Angel Falls. Her eyelids felt heavy, her joints ached, her chest burned, and even her teeth hurt. She realized, just before sleep overcame her, that she was sick.

Inconvenient, she thought drowsily. It was a lucky thing she'd already talked with Maggie, gotten rid of Gabriel. She could take care of herself.

It was a simple fever. A case of the flu. It was no wonder she was imagining herself falling in love with the beautiful stranger who'd arrived in their midst. No wonder that she started seeing Emerson MacVey in him, when the two were as different as night and day.

She needed fluids, plenty of rest and quiet. In a few days she'd be her old self, full of energy, compassion, and not a trace of wistful longing for something that would only bring her pain.

In a few days, everything would be just fine.

Chapter Eleven

So he'd saved her life. Why wasn't that good enough? If she'd been driving when the brakes on her car failed, she probably would have ended up against that tree. So he'd taken care of his first duty, hadn't he? Why did he feel he wasn't through with Carrie Alexander? Maybe because he didn't want to be.

Gabriel maneuvered Lars's truck up the steep, icy driveway, put it into Park and turned it off. It was dark already, and through the brightly lit windows of the old Victorian-style house he could see the family bustling around, all energy and life. A life at which he could only be a spectator.

It was odd. When he'd been alive he hadn't cared about holidays, about family, about friends, even. His parents had divorced and remarried so many times he'd almost lost track of who had actually produced him thirty-two years ago. He'd sat through all the sentimental Christmas movies, listened to all the treacly Christmas songs, and never given a damn.

He did now. He wanted that warmth, that family. He wanted cinnamon rolls dripping with butter, not nouvelle cuisine. He wanted American beer, not

French wine. He wanted friends and family, he wanted life. He wanted sex. And he wanted love.

Three people whose lives he'd ruined. Carrie Alexander was number one, and he ought to feel vindicated. He'd saved her life, lectured her on the error of her ways and been summarily banished. If she had any sense she'd pull herself together, head back for a city and shake the dust from this dying town.

Even if she wouldn't, he was no longer to blame. He could forget about her, about her luminous blue eyes and corn-silk hair, her soft mouth and too-thin body that needed pasta and cinnamon buns, as well. Forget how much he wanted to touch her again.

It was now abundantly clear to him just who number two was. He'd ruined the lives of the entire population of Angel Falls, no mean feat for a shallow yuppie. Augusta couldn't be expecting him to fix everyone, but he had little doubt he was living with Lars Swensen for a reason. If he could do something about the Swensens, somehow right the wrong he'd done Lars, then maybe he'd be ready to move on.

He still had no inkling who number three might be, and at that moment he didn't really care. He was tired, still shaken from the near miss in Carrie's rust-bucket of a car, and tense from a frustration that was a great deal more than sexual. He wanted to go up to his room, lock the door and slam his fist against the wall.

But one month didn't allow for wasted time. When he walked into the warmth and light of the old kitchen, baby Carrie looked up at him with a beaming, toothless grin, Lars clapped him on the back, and even Maggie's careworn face warmed at the sight of him.

For a moment he wanted to yell at them. They were fools to trust him—he was the man who'd brought them to this point in the first place. But even if he wanted to tell them, he wouldn't be able to—he'd already discovered that any attempt to tell someone the truth about who and what he was ended in silence.

And he was no longer sure who and what he was. Gabriel Falconi had taken over, Emerson MacVey was fading fast, and like the rest of MacVey's acquaintances, he couldn't mourn him. He was a cold, heartless man, better off dead. And from what little he could see from the time he'd been back on earth, he didn't deserve heaven.

"I need your help, Gabriel," Lars boomed out from his place at the head of the scrubbed table. He had an omnipresent cup of coffee in one big hand, and Gabriel accepted his own from Maggie with automatic thanks. "I'm working on a mahogany railing, and I need it done by Christmas. I don't know how much Carrie has for you, but if you'd feel like giving me a hand..."

"Carrie doesn't need me out there for a few days," he said, wondering if it was a lie. He had the sense, probably wishful thinking on his part, that she needed him very badly. "I'd be glad to help."

"I'll pay you, of course," Lars said carefully. "I'm not sure how much I have right now..."

"Pay me when you get paid," Gabriel replied easily. "I have all that I need right now. A warm place to live, good food, friends..." The moment the word left his mouth it shocked him, but fortunately Lars was too relieved to notice his surprise. He'd never before considered that he had friends.

"We work well together," Lars said. "I wish you could see your way clear to staying past the New Year. I'm doing this railing on spec at the moment, but if we just had a little luck I think we could make a modest go of it."

"Luck," Maggie said with a snort from her spot at the stove. "A Christmas miracle is more like it."

Thank you, Augusta, Gabriel said silently. "Miracles have been known to happen," he drawled, drinking his strong coffee and wondering how he'd ever liked tea.

He didn't even think of Carrie for the next few days. At least, not more than once or twice an hour. And all night long, in his dreams, in his waking, in his drifting off to sleep. Instead he concentrated on the long sweep of carved mahogany railing, the hand-carved newel posts that filled most of Lars's workshop. And he concentrated on his Christmas miracle.

In the end he was afraid he'd wasted it.

Alexander Borodin was a millionaire, patron of the arts, industrialist, with an eye for talent. Emerson MacVey had despised him as a sentimental old fool with a weakness for antiquated ways of doing things. Borodin specialized in restoring old mansions with lovingly detailed woodwork—MacVey had preferred chrome and steel.

But Borodin had connections throughout the world—he would see the rare beauty in Lars's work, and he could easily provide enough commissions to keep the Swensen family happily solvent into the millennium and beyond. Last Emerson had heard, he was in the midst of investing in a chain of small, exclusive hotels throughout the world, renovated from some of the small palaces and manor houses that had fallen on hard times. Lars's gift would prove invaluable.

But actually getting in touch with Borodin proved to be no easy matter. Alexander Borodin was not the sort of man one simply called—you had to wade through secretaries and assistants and vice presidents and administrators, and each one had very strong reasons not to let you talk to the man.

One name would have done the trick, opened the lines of communication instantly, but it was a name Gabriel was unable to speak. It was just as well. No one would have believed him anyway.

Three days of trying to reach him, three days of running up long-distance phone bills that would probably rival the national debt, three days of being on hold, and Gabriel had simply closed his eyes, focused on Augusta's stern face, and silently asked.

A moment later Alexander Borodin's accented voice came on the line. "I gather you've been trying to reach me, young man. What can I do for you?"

After that it was simple enough. No more miracles were required—Gabriel discovered he was fluent enough when he cared to be persuasive, and it didn't take much to persuade Borodin to look at some of Lars's work. Lars had an old camera, Angel Falls came equipped with a one-hour developing service and the U.S. postal service had express mail. The deed was as good as done.

Two down, Gabriel thought, wondering if he should go see Gertrude. He'd been assiduously avoiding her for the past few days, not ready to look at those thick glasses and know the power of a coldhearted eternity lay behind them. He'd have to face her sooner or later. For now, he was content to keep his distance.

Oddly enough, the one person he missed, aside from Carrie, was Jeffie. After their brief run-in at the market, he'd wanted to call him, to talk to him, but he couldn't find a reasonable excuse. And Jeffie, who apparently used to haunt the Swensens' house, was making himself alarmingly scarce.

Probably sulking after being caught trying to shoplift, Gabriel thought, but he didn't quite believe it. For some reason Jeffie seemed to take his strictures with an almost pathetic gratitude. There'd been none of the expected sullen defiance at the store, just a look of such guilt and misery that it almost broke Gabriel's heart.

"Seen Jeffie recently?" he'd managed to ask Nils one day in what he hoped was a suitably offhand voice.

Nils had shrugged. "I saw him in school the other day. He's doing okay, I guess. I asked him if he wanted to come over, work in the shop, but he said no. Said he didn't have anyone to make presents for."

"Poor baby," Maggie had murmured. "Lars, you should go see him."

Lars had set down his paper. "After church on Sunday, Maggie," he agreed. "We'll invite him to dinner, and we won't take no for an answer. It'll give him a chance to talk with Gabe. He seems to think you're some kind of hero," he said with comfortable amusement.

And Gabriel, knowing he should protest, simply nodded, dismissing his unreasoning sense of foreboding.

The days passed with no word from Carrie, and Gabriel worked in the shop beside Lars and told himself his work was done. He'd have no reason to see her again, no reason to talk to her, to touch her. He'd saved her life. Surely things were even now.

And even if Borodin had yet to be in touch, Gabriel had little doubt it would work out. It would take a fool not to see the sheer artistry in Lars's work, and Borodin had never been a fool.

It wasn't until Sunday that Gabriel began to admit to the uneasiness that had been gnawing away at him. An uneasiness that was reflected in Lars's face. Carrie wasn't in church.

"Don't tell me she never misses church," he said, unbelieving as they made their way down the icy church steps. Kirsten had her hand clasped firmly in his, something he was getting dangerously used to.

"Not if she can help it. And certainly not during Advent," Maggie said. "Carrie lives for Christmas. I'm going out to see her once we get home."

"I'll go," Gabriel said, in a voice that brooked no opposition.

Maggie looked at him for a long, considering moment, her face troubled. "I don't think..."

A new voice came from directly behind him. "Let Gabriel go."

Gabriel froze. He'd managed to avoid Gertrude, telling himself he wasn't ready to deal with her. He should have known it wouldn't be up to him.

He turned and looked down at her, at the hunched-over, delicate old-lady figure, the bottle-glass lenses shielding those too-sharp eyes, the kindly expression on her face that masked the look of judge and jury.

"Is she all right?" he demanded sharply.

"I have no idea, young man," Gertrude said sweetly. "I'm just a bit of a matchmaker at heart."

"Go ahead," Lars said, clamping a heavy hand on his shoulder. "Take the truck, and give us a call when you get there. Maggie will save some Sunday dinner for you."

He didn't hesitate any longer. The past few days had been bitter cold, with a wind that blew down from Canada and chilled to the bone. The snow on the roads was packed, sanded, and he drove much too fast toward Carrie's decrepit little farmhouse, all the while telling himself he was ridiculous to be worried, telling himself he should have let Maggie go, should have suggested Maggie at least call, should have got on with the business of finding out who his third soul to save was. He was finished with Carrie, damn it! He'd managed to resist temptation, to do no more than kiss her. He'd saved her life—surely they were quits?

The moment the house came in view all his foreboding tripled. Carrie's car was sitting out front— Steve must have fixed it and brought it back to her, a hell of a lot faster than he was getting around to fixing his truck. But the house looked dark, deserted. And there was no wood smoke coming from the chimney.

He knew for a fact that Carrie had no source of backup heat. All she had was that damnable wood stove in her living room, and on a cold December day if there was no smoke coming from the chimney then there was no heat in the house.

He skidded down the driveway, slammed Lars's truck into Park and jumped out. Her front door was locked, but panic was riding him so hard that he simply kicked it open with his unexpected strength, splintering the wooden frame.

"Carrie!" he shouted. There was no answer. And the homey little kitchen was icy cold.

He slammed the door behind him, but it bounced back open again, letting in a blast of arctic air. He grabbed a chair and shoved it against the door, then raced into the living room.

If he'd had ten years left to live, the sight of her would have taken them off his life. She was lying on the sofa, still and cold, cocooned in a pile of old quilts, with a weak electric heater putting out barely a teaspoonful of heat in the icy room. For a moment he froze, certain she was dead. And then he heard the noisy rasp of her breathing.

He began to curse under his breath, furiously, obscenely, and in Italian. He didn't even take time to be surprised by that fact, as he rushed across the room and knelt by Carrie's unconscious figure. She was burning up with fever, and she stirred under his hand, murmuring something out of dried lips, something he couldn't hear.

The wood box was empty, of course, and obviously she'd been too sick to deal with the fire. His fury vanished into some dark cold place inside him as he sprang into action. It took him ten seconds and one terse sentence to get Lars to find a doctor, and then he concentrated on the wood box. By the time cars started arriving he'd managed to get a roaring fire going, bringing the temperature of the house up to a balmy fifty-five degrees. And Carrie hadn't moved.

He didn't know the man who rushed in with Maggie, but the sight of the black bag did wonders for his barely controlled state of panic. "Doc Browning," Maggie muttered a hurried introduction. "This is Gabriel. Where is she?"

"In the living room. I think it's pneumonia."

Doc Browning, an elderly little urchin of a man with long, tufted eyebrows, looked at him in surprise. "Even without seeing her, I imagine you're probably right," he said. "I warned her." He started into the living room, muttering under his breath. "She needs fluids. Make her warm too."

"The pipes are frozen," Gabriel said dourly. "I'll see what I can do."

There was frozen water in the kettle on the gas stove. He turned on all the burners, hoping to add even a trace of warmth to the frigid house, and then went back to the living room.

He stopped in the doorway. Doc Browning was sitting on the sofa beside Carrie, listening to her breathe. He'd unfastened the shirt she wore, and Gabriel could see her pale skin, the soft curve of her breasts, and he knew he was going to hell for sure, to be lusting after a woman who might very well be dying.

And hell couldn't be that much worse than being around Carrie Alexander and not touching her.

"It's pneumonia, all right," Doc Browning said, pulling her shirt closed again. "She's burning with fever, she's dehydrated, she's too damned thin, and if I had any sense I'd take her to the hospital."

"You can't, Doc," Maggie said. "She doesn't have insurance."

"If she needs the hospital..." Gabriel began.

"We can give it a day," Doc said wearily. "I know Carrie—she hates like hell to be beholden to anyone. She wouldn't take charity, and hospitals don't like to give it. If someone can stay with her, make sure she gets her medicine, fluids, keeps warm, then I can wait a day. These things usually respond to antibiotics quickly."

"I'll stay," Maggie said. "We took care of her last time."

"No," Gabriel said in a calm, sure voice. "I'll stay."

"But she needs a woman to look after her..."

"I don't think she cares much about modesty at this point, Maggie," Doc Browning said. "And Gabriel here is a lot stronger than you are. Besides, someone's got to do something about the water situation. And you're still nursing, and no way am I having that baby come into a sick house."

Maggie was defeated, and she knew it. She took it with good grace. "We'll bring dinner out," she said to Gabriel. "And Lars can come help with the frozen pipes."

Gabriel nodded, staring at Carrie's still figure. Her cheeks were bright red with fever, the rest of her was almost marble white, and it took all his effort to keep his rage and fear under control. She couldn't die, damn it! He refused to let her. And not for any fear for his own eternity. He'd accepted the fact that he deserved hell and would probably end up there.

But Carrie was a different matter. She wouldn't even have to pause at the Waystation. She'd be on an express train straight to heaven, and he'd never see her again.

So he damned well wasn't going to let her go too soon.

Doc Browning was rummaging around in his leather bag. "I'm going to start her with a double dose of penicillin, but after that it's going to be up to you to see that she gets it down. Every six hours, regular as clockwork, and pump those fluids into her. Herb teas, fruit juice, ginger ale. Nothing with caffeine—it'll dry her out even more. You think you're up to it?" He fixed Gabriel with a fierce stare.

"I'm up to it."

Browning nodded, satisfied. "What the hell is this town going to do when I'm out of here?" he demanded of no one in particular.

"You're leaving?" Gabriel asked.

"The whole town's dying. Can't afford to be a doctor for a hundred people—I've got to go where I'm needed. In another month Carrie wouldn't have any choice—you'd have had to drive her to the emergency room." He rose, staring down at her.

"We're just glad you're still here, Doc," Maggie said.

"Hell and damnation!" the old man exploded. "I warned her. She's going to kill herself if she keeps on this way. Never taking care of herself, not eating decent meals, not getting enough sleep. She's run-down, too damned skinny, and this house is as drafty as a gazebo. It's no wonder she's sick."

"I'll take care of the house," Gabriel said. "And I'll take care of her."

Doc just looked at him. And then he smiled, a faint, wintry smile. "I believe you will. Come along, Maggie. We're leaving her in good hands."

Gabriel wasn't so sure. By the time the water in the kettle had melted and begun to boil he'd loaded the wood box with enough firewood to keep the stove going for a couple of days. The temperature had risen to a comfortable level, and he took the electric heater into the bathroom and aimed it at the pipes, giving them a head start, before he made a pot of apple cinnamon tea.

Carrie was burning up when he brought her a cup, laced with honey. She'd kicked off her covers, and she was muttering something underneath her breath, something he couldn't begin to make out. He knelt beside her on the floor, put his arm under her shoulders to raise her, and put the mug to her cracked lips.

She took an instinctive, automatic sip, and he was careful not to let her choke. She drank half the cup slowly and then her eyes fluttered open, fever bright, to stare at him in shocked disbelief.

She tried to say something, but she had no voice beyond a whisper. And then she closed her eyes again, and he set her back on the couch, covering her frail body up once more with the quilt.

If she was going to recuperate here and not in the hospital, they'd need water. He rose, staring down at her, loath to even leave the room. She looked marginally better now, though it was probably only wishful thinking on his part. She wasn't going to die. She was going to sleep, long, healing sleep, while he got the house in working order again. And then he was going to come back into the living room and sit there and watch her. Just watch her. Indulge himself in the sheer, hopeless pleasure of it. Knowing that he only had a couple of weeks left.

THE DREAMS WERE extraordinary. Fever bright, a whirl of colors, dancing around in her head. Once she gave in to them the fear left her, and she drifted like a leaf on the wind through the magic, willingly, the heat and the cold wrapping her in a tight cocoon of forgetfulness.

And then they came, pulling at her, poking at her, forcing things down her throat, and she wanted to tell them all to go away. Until she opened her eyes and saw him through the crystalline haze. And for the first time in years everything felt right again.

She wanted to tell him. She wanted to reach out and touch him, but she was too weak. She couldn't even keep her eyes open, to stare at him in wonder. She felt herself sink back, and she fought it for a moment, terrified he'd leave her once more.

But he wouldn't. She knew that with a certainty. He'd be there, watching over her, taking care of her, for as long as she needed. She didn't have to fight anymore. She was no longer alone.

She could hear him moving around in the kitchen, banging on the pipes. She could feel him all around her. Even behind her closed eyelids she could watch him as he put more wood on the stove, sending blankets of heat through the house. She was cold, chilled, but he seemed to sense that, for he tucked the quilt around her, and brushed the hair away from her face, and she wanted to look at him again, she wanted to tell him she knew him, she wanted to cry.

But there were no tears, no words. She simply slept, secure in the knowledge that he'd come to her when she most needed it. And she never had to be lonely again.

When she woke it was dark. The room was warm, and there was a light on in the kitchen, spreading a pool of illumination into the shadowy living room. There was no sound but the quiet crackle of the wood fire, and she wondered whether she was alone. He'd fed her a second dose of medicine and more tea, and she knew she had to go to the bathroom, but she wasn't sure if she'd manage to crawl. The pipes were frozen, she remembered that. She'd tried to thaw them, but she hadn't the strength—she'd just lain on the couch and coughed.

No, she wasn't alone. She could feel him in the house, nearby. If she turned her head she'd seen him watching over her. Like a guardian angel, protecting her while she fought the monster that squatted on her chest, heavy and smothering. Her mouth moved in a faint smile at the notion, and she heard him move, coming to her side, and she knew he was watching her out of those beautiful dark brown eyes.

She opened her own and smiled up at him, dreaming, fevered, peaceful. "I thought you were dead, Emerson," she whispered. And then she slept again.

GABRIEL DIDN'T MOVE. He was kneeling beside her, one of her hot, dry hands in his large ones, and he was the one who felt chilled.

There had been calm lucidity in her eyes. Despite the fever raging in her frail body, she'd looked into his eyes and seen him, known him, and the thought shattered him in ways he couldn't bear to contemplate. Most of all because he found he didn't want to be Emerson MacVey, ever again.

Why the hell had she loved him? The man he once was had been a shallow, manipulative bastard, capable of destroying a town on a whim, capable of bedding and discarding a vulnerable young woman without even having the guts to do it face-to-face. Emerson MacVey hadn't been mourned when he'd come to his untimely end, and Gabriel Falconi knew why. He'd been merciless, and he deserved no mercy shown toward him.

But Carrie had loved him. Carrie, who seemed to have enough love for all the lost, needy creatures of this earth, Carrie who had enough love for everyone but herself. Carrie had loved him. And that knowledge was his one saving grace.

He sat back on his heels, staring at her in the shadowy darkness. He'd managed to get the water going—the pipes had burst under the kitchen sink but he could wash the dishes in the bathtub until he replaced them. Lars and Maggie had brought dinner out as promised, staying long enough to worry over Carrie. And now they were alone, he with his guilt and his misplaced desire, she with her fever dreams.

She was shivering, and he knew what that meant. Her fever was spiking again, climbing to dangerous levels, despite all the aspirin he'd poured down her throat. The antibiotic wouldn't start kicking in for at least another few hours, and all he could do was sit there and watch her burn up with fever.

The shivering became shaking. Her skin was scorching, and her eyes opened again, glazed, unseeing, and she began to mutter lost, hopeless words that tore him apart.

He rose, and she clawed at him. "Don't," she whispered in a raw thread of a voice. "Don't leave again." And he didn't know whether she was talking to Gabriel. Or Emerson.

It didn't matter. "I'll be right back," he murmured, stroking her forehead.

It took forever to fill the bathtub with cool water. When he couldn't wait anymore he went back to get her. She was thrashing around, the covers kicked to the floor, and her flannel nightgown was tangled around her long dancer's legs.

He carried her into the bathroom, settling her into the tub, nightgown and all. She jerked in his arms from the shock of the cool water, making a quiet moan of distress, and he felt unexpected tears burn his eyes. He wanted her better. He wanted her to turn suddenly clear, lucid eyes on him and demand to know why she was sitting in a bathtub full of cold water with her nightgown on. He wanted a miracle.

"Augusta, damn it," he muttered. "Or God. I don't care who. Just fix her. Somebody. Make her better. Now."

But this time there was no instant miracle. Carrie's eyes were tightly shut, and she was crying, shaking from cold and fever, and suddenly Gabriel couldn't stand it any longer. He scooped her up, stripped the sopping nightgown from her, wrapped a thick towel around her and carried her back into the living room. He dumped her onto the sofa and threw the quilts over her, staring down at her as she fell back asleep. And then he grabbed his coat and headed out the door.

He'd send Maggie back, he told himself as the chill night air bit into lungs. Or Lars could drive her to the hospital, and Gabriel could use that amazing gold credit card that would never come due. He had to get away from her—he couldn't help her, couldn't save her, and couldn't live with the guilt of watching her as she struggled to breathe.

He yanked at the door to the truck, climbing inside. He had to get away, run away, like the damned coward he was, and had always been. If he'd wondered whether he was Emerson or Gabriel there was no longer any question. Carrie had looked at him through fever-bright eyes and known him. Emerson was the make who'd abandon a desperately ill woman in the middle of the night. Emerson was the ultimate coward who'd run away from all responsibilities, all caring, all emotion.

He reached for the key, and then his hand dropped, and he put his head on the steering wheel, feeling the shame and guilt wash over him. "Please," he said out loud, not knowing whom he was asking, or even what. "Please," he said again, his voice hoarse and breaking.

This time there was an answer. This was his second miracle, wasted on his own worthless self. Not a miracle for Carrie, to make her instantly better. But the strength for him, to deal with it.

Prayers are always answered, the minister had said, just this morning, and yet it seemed like centuries ago that he'd sat in the little Lutheran church, so consumed with worry about Carrie that he thought he hadn't even been listening. Prayers are answered, but you just might not get the answer you want.

And sometimes you get what you need, Gabriel thought, closing the door silently behind him and staring around Carrie's kitchen. Dumping his jacket onto one of the chairs, he moved silently back into the living room. Carrie lay on the sofa, unmoving, her cheeks still flushed with fever.

And Gabriel sank down on the floor beside the sofa, prepared for a night-long vigil.

Chapter Twelve

Carrie was warm. Cosily, comfortably warm, not burning hot. The pain in her chest had lessened, and as she snuggled down further into the soft mattress she knew an unexpected sense of rightness. She opened her eyes warily, seeing the early-morning light filling her bedroom, and then she turned her head.

Gabriel was asleep beside her. In the dawn she could see the lines of exhaustion on his beautiful face, the scruffy growth of beard. He was wearing jeans and a T-shirt, nothing more, and he lay sprawled out on her double bed, filling it.

She couldn't resist. She lifted her hand, noticing that it was trembling, and touched his mouth with her fingertips.

He murmured something, but he didn't wake up, and Carrie almost leaned forward and touched him with her lips, as well. In time sanity reared its ugly head, and she pulled back, sliding out of the bed silently as Gabriel slept on.

She could barely stand, her legs felt so weak. She glanced down at her body, noting that she was wearing an old T-shirt and nothing else. She hadn't put that T-shirt on her body.

She had hazy memories, of Gabriel putting her in the bathtub, of holding her in his arms as he rocked by the wood stove, of tea and soup and medicine being forced down her throat. At one point Doc Browning had been there, she was sure she'd heard his voice, and the Swensens had come, as well.

But through it all Gabriel had remained, watching over her, taking care of her, a presence, along with her fever dreams. Her fever dreams of Emerson MacVey.

It made no sense that the two of them should be so mixed up in her head. There were never two more dissimilar men. But maybe it all boiled down to one constant. In both cases, she'd made the dire mistake of being stupidly, irrationally attracted to the wrong man.

She had to hold on to the wall as she made her way down the hallway to the bathroom. She looked at her reflection in the mirror and shuddered. She looked like death warmed over. Her face was pinched and pale, her eyes huge in her face, her hair a rat's nest. She needed to use the toilet, she needed to brush her teeth, and she needed to wash her hair.

Her strength held out until halfway through her shower, and then she sagged against the metal side of the stall, too weary to move, trying to summon up enough energy to even turn off the water. She barely heard the door open, and then Gabriel was there, filling the room.

"You're crazy," he said. And then he calmly stepped into the shower with her, turned off the spray and scooped her trembling, wet body up into his arms.

Wrapping her in a towel, he carried her back into the bedroom, setting her down gently on the bed. She was able to gather enough strength to bat his hands away when he began to dry her off with efficient, impersonal care. She didn't want him to be impersonal.

"I can do it," she said crossly.

He smiled. He was wet from the shower, water stains across the dark T-shirt he wore, and his face was weary beneath his good humor. He looked as if he'd been to hell and back. "I wasn't sure that antibiotic was ever going to work."

The towel was huge, enveloping, and he was hardly likely to be tempted by her skinny, unfeminine body, but she wrapped it tightly around her anyway. "How long have I been sick?"

"Years. Centuries," he said. "Actually, I don't know. I found you on Sunday, and today's...God, I think it's Tuesday, but I could be wrong."

"Have you been here all this time? Taking care of me?"

"Yes." He put his hand on her forehead and frowned slightly. "I think your fever's about gone, but maybe I'd better check. Taking a shower was a damned stupid thing to do when you can barely walk. Why did you?"

She was too exhausted to think about what she was saying. "Because I looked horrible," she blurted out.

He stared at her for a brief, astonished moment. And then he threw back his head and laughed.

Carrie scrambled beneath the covers, mortally offended. "It's not funny," she said sulkily.

He leaned forward, kneeling on the bed beside her, his hands cupping her face, his long fingers sliding through her wet hair. "No," he agreed, "it's wonderful. I thought you were too busy being the saint of Angel Falls to waste a precious moment on yourself."

"I'm not a saint."

"No," he said. "And you look wonderful." And he leaned forward and kissed her.

It was a revelation of a kiss. Tender, without being the slightest bit platonic, his mouth touched hers, clinging, warm and damp, and she felt the heat building in her. Something had changed while she'd been sick, something had shifted inside her, and she wanted this man. Wanted him enough to risk taking him.

She lifted her arms, but he'd already stepped away, unaware of her longing. "I'll make you some tea," he said briskly, "and toast, and maybe some applesauce. If you can manage that then maybe we can graduate to eggs."

"I'm not hungry," she said, trying to squash her longing. "And I want coffee."

"Too bad. If you eat enough to satisfy me then maybe I'll let you have a little bit of coffee. Maybe not." He looked down at her, a considering light in his eyes. "You stay put. If you want to get dressed I'll help you, after you have something to eat."

"I can take care of it myself."

"Trust me, Carrie, I've seen you without a stitch on any number of times during the past few days."

"I'm sure you can control your raging passions," she said sharply, "but I want my privacy."

He halted by the door, staring at her. "I wouldn't be sure of any such thing," he said with a crooked smile. "Stay put."

There was something about his smile. Something about the look in his eyes, that made her start wondering whether there might be a future for her after all.

SHE DIDN'T DO as he told her to, but then, Gabriel hadn't expected it. To everyone else she was Lady Bountiful, the saint, the martyr, ready to sacrifice everything for her fellow man. When it came to him she was stubborn, determined and sharp-tongued. He wondered whether it was love.

He hoped not. He'd saved her life twice, above and beyond the call of duty. Surely by now he was quits. He didn't think Augusta would look too kindly on things if Carrie fell in love with him, only to have him vanish in two weeks' time.

He thought about her mouth, tasting of toothpaste and longing. Of her huge eyes, staring up at him with such a troubled expression in their blue depths. He thought of her skinny body that needed food and love and sex, and he thought it just might be worth it. He'd already been here half his allotted time and it didn't seem as if he'd made any progress at all. Maybe he ought to take what he wanted and prepare to spend eternity in hell. Since he seemed bound there anyway, he might as well have something to remember.

He'd do it, too, if it was only his eternity he had to consider. But Carrie had been through enough. She'd already been used and rejected by Emerson MacVey. If Gabriel entered into an affair with her, knowing it was doomed, then he'd deserve any torment fate could offer him.

It took all his self-control not to go to her when she appeared in the kitchen door, swaying slightly, dressed, triumphant, pale. He wanted to put his arms around her, he wanted to carry her back up to bed, he wanted to make love to her.

He contented himself with glancing her way, then turning back to the stove. "I knew you wouldn't stay put," he said. "I've got the fire cranked up. Go lie down on the sofa and I'll bring you something to eat."

"Are you always this dictatorial?"

He grinned. "Only when I get the chance. Are you always this crabby?"

Her slow, answering smile was a revelation. "Only when I get the chance."

She ate everything he put in front of her, then demanded coffee. Faint color began to reappear in her cheeks, and by the time the Swensens' car pulled up the long, icy driveway she was arguing about who was going to do the dishes.

"It's a miracle," Maggie breathed when she rushed into the room, not taking time to discard her coat. "Yesterday you were at death's door and now you look like the cat that swallowed the canary."

"I told you she'd be all right," Lars said, coming in behind her, his broad face creased with pleasure. "She was in good hands with our Gabriel. A hospital would have been a waste of time and money."

He heard the phrase, "our Gabriel," and the warmth of it sent a shaft of sorrow through him, for the connections he'd never made when he had the chance. He squashed it down—it was too late for recriminations. "You need coffee," he drawled. "I'll get it, while you see if you can put the patient in a more agreeable mood."

Both the Swensens turned to look at Carrie in surprise. "Carrie's always agreeable," Maggie said.

"Of course I am," Carrie said. "Except when a bully like Gabriel tries to boss me around."

Lars looked at Maggie, and the two of them grinned. Gabriel knew what they were thinking, and he wanted to tell them to stop it. There was nothing worth grinning about—he was bad for her, the worst possible man. He could offer her sex and desertion, and she deserved love and commitment.

"Coffee," he said morosely, disappearing into the kitchen.

The day was a stream of visitors. Everyone brought something. Food, flowers, homemade tokens. Gabriel kept himself out of the way, busy with making the drafty old house more secure against the harsh December winds. He caulked windows, fixed the banking on the west side of the house, and was in the midst of stacking firewood when he had an uneasy prickling sensation at the back of his neck. He knew who it was even before he turned.

"You're running out of time, Gabriel," said Gertrude Hansen in Augusta's peremptory tones.

He paused, leaning on the splitting maul, and looked down at her. Emerson had been the same height as Augusta, but here in Minnesota he was taller and she was shorter. He didn't bother pretending to misunderstand. "I have two weeks left."

"And what have you done so far?"

"Saved Carrie's life. Twice. Surely that's enough."

"Could be," the old lady murmured. "It all depends on what kind of state you leave her in. She doesn't need her heart broken again."

"I'm not going to touch her," he snapped.

The old lady just looked at him. "We'll see," she said obscurely, moving past him onto the porch just as Lars and Maggie came out.

"Hi, there, Gertrude," Lars said. "Come to see the invalid? You wouldn't believe how well she's doing. Gabriel's a miracle worker."

Gertrude directed a sour glance back at him. "Is he?" she murmured in the deceptively gentle voice that fooled the Swensens, a far cry from Augusta's autocratic tones. "I would have thought he was the type to save his miracles for himself."

Guilt swamped him, leaving him speechless as Gertrude disappeared inside the house. She was right, damn it. His miracle had been for himself, for his miserable, cowardly self.

"She's an old tartar sometimes," Lars said, putting a hand on Gabriel's shoulder. "Don't pay any attention to her. We've known her all her life, and we're used to her."

It was enough to startle him out of his abstraction. "I thought she was new in town."

"What made you think that?" Maggie asked, perplexed. "She was born here, and as far as I know she's never even left the state in all her eighty-some years."

Gabriel shook his head. Trust Augusta to take care of details. "Just a guess," he said. "How's Carrie doing? Is she getting overtired?"

"Hell, she's fine," Lars boomed, then silenced as Maggie kicked him.

"She's doing quite well," Maggie corrected him, "but I don't think she ought to be left alone. Would you mind staying here a little bit longer?"

It was the last thing he needed, and what he wanted most. The longer he was around her, the harder it was for him to resist her. And resist her was the one thing he had to do. If he hadn't known it already, Gertrude's warning had reminded him.

"She's got enough food to feed the Russian army," he said. "Her fever's normal..."

"She needs you, Gabriel," Maggie said gently.

He wanted to deny it. He wanted to explain to Maggie just how dangerous he was to Carrie Alexander's fragile well-being, but he knew it was a waste of time. "Of course I'll stay," he said, hating the savage relief he felt at having to agree.

"In the excitement, I forgot to tell you," Lars was saying, "someone's coming to look at the railings. He might be interested in commissioning some other work."

"He's got a Russian-sounding name. Something like Boris Gudonov," Maggie said.

"Borodin," Lars corrected her. "His name's Alexander Borodin. He must have money—he's using his own jet to fly into Saint Cloud."

Gabriel closed his eyes for a moment, offering up a silent prayer of thankfulness. "I've heard of him," he said carefully. "If he likes your stuff you've got it made."

"Let's not count our chickens," Maggie said, but she sounded a great deal more cheerful than she had in the past few weeks. She put her hand on Gabriel's arm, and her eyes were suddenly dark with concern. "Do you really not want to stay here, Gabriel? I could come out, or Gertrude, or any number of people would leap at the chance to do something for Carrie, after all she's done for us."

"I'll stay," Gabriel said, putting his hand over Maggie's work-worn one. "I want to."

But he wasn't about to go back into the house as long as Gertrude was there, and she stayed a damnably long time. The sky grew dark early as they neared the shortest day of the year, and he could sense another winter storm in the air, he who'd never paid the slightest bit of attention to the weather. The temperature was dropping, he'd left his jacket inside, and there was a limit to how much wood he could split and stack before his energy gave out. He'd been through two days of hell, two days of panic, spooning medicine and soup and tea down Carrie's throat, moving her from bed to bath and back again, all the while cursing Augusta and the fate that had put her life in his hands. He'd barely slept or eaten since Sunday, and he wanted to sit by the wood stove and look at Carrie. With no one interfering.

"You can go in now." Gertrude strode out the door, her cloth coat buttoned up under her wattled chin, her thick glasses glinting in the waning sunlight. "You behave yourself now. She tires easily."

"I have no intention of tiring her," he said sourly.

Gertrude's smile was no more warming than the weather. "I don't trust you, Gabriel," she said. "You'll have to prove yourself to me." And before he could reply, she was gone, zipping off at an alarmingly fast rate in her sturdy sedan.

He watched her go. "At least she called me Gabriel," he muttered out loud. Right then and there he didn't want to be reminded of who he once was, and would be again in another couple of weeks.

Carrie was fast asleep on the living room sofa. Someone, probably Lars, had loaded the wood stove, and the heat was wonderful after the chill winter air. Gabriel poured himself a cup of coffee, took a brownie from the plate someone had brought that morning, and took a seat by the fire, where he could watch Carrie. He didn't know why fate had given him one more night with her. He only knew it would be his last chance. And he intended to make the most of it. By watching her, simply watching her. So that he'd have something to remember, throughout eternity. Wherever he ended up.

IT WAS AN INTERESTING phenomenon, lusting after a man. Carrie had more than enough time to consider it, advantages, disadvantages and all. In her twenty-seven years she'd never been unduly interested in men. Her sexual experience consisted of a vaguely unsatisfying short-term affair with a fellow student, and the cataclysmic night she'd spent in Emerson MacVey's office.

She'd sworn off sex after that. Sworn off men, relationships, dating, and doing just about anything else a normal, healthy young woman might be interested in doing. Most men, including Steve from the garage, had taken no for an answer. The sexless aura she put forth had been astonishingly convincing.

She wasn't quite sure why it hadn't convinced Gabriel. From his sudden appearance in her life, she'd gone out of her way to be motherly, asexual, a friend and nothing more. But he had a way of seeing through that, of getting under her skin, so that she was aware of him constantly, as she'd been aware of no other man.

She ought to bless the fact that her responses were normal, healthy ones. After all, Gabriel was a devastatingly attractive man, quiet, strong, with a streak of ironic humor that matched her own. He was only going to be around for another few weeks—what could be wrong with indulging her unexpected longings?

She'd gotten support from the most unexpected quarter. Gertrude, maiden schoolteacher and pillar of the community, had taken one look at her and shaken her head.

"It's not the things you do that you regret," she'd murmured, following Carrie's glance out the window toward Gabriel as he stacked firewood with his graceful economy of movement. "It's the things you don't do."

Carrie had turned to look at her, scandalized. "He's leaving in two weeks, Gertrude."

"When did you last do something for yourself? Something just because you wanted to do it, and to hell with the consequences?"

"Are you telling me to have an affair?" Carrie demanded. "Gertrude, you were my seventh-grade social studies teacher!"

"I'm telling you to do what your heart tells you," Gertrude had said placidly. "Nothing more. And nothing less."

But it wasn't her heart talking to her, Carrie thought, staring at Gabriel across the table as she ate more pasta than she'd eaten in the past year. It was something a lot more elemental. She watched his hands, strong, elegant hands that he'd put on her more than once, and she wondered how she could entice him to put them on her again. She looked at his mouth, wide, mobile. That mouth had kissed her when she wasn't sure that she wanted to be kissed.

This time she was sure. But she didn't know how to get him to kiss her.

And damn it, he was keeping his distance, fussing around her like a mother hen, as deliberately asexual as she had been. It was almost as if their roles had been reversed. Suddenly she wanted him to see her as a woman, not a plaster saint. And suddenly, he was coming on like Francis of Assisi.

"You should go to bed," he said when she finished off her third brownie. "You need to rebuild your strength." He began clearing the table, keeping well out of her way, almost as if he suspected she might grab him.

Tempting thought. "I've spent the past week in bed," she countered, rising to help him. "I feel restless."

He turned in the doorway, and she almost ran into him. They were breathlessly, deliciously close, close enough for her to feel the heat from his body, close enough to see the flicker of reaction in his beautiful brown eyes, a reaction he banished so quickly she wondered if it was wishful thinking on her part.

"Are you afraid of me, Gabriel?" she asked suddenly, artlessly.

"Why should I be?"

"You seem to be running away from me," she murmured, beginning to enjoy herself.

"I didn't know there was anything to run from."

She took the plate from his hand and put it on the adjacent counter. "There isn't."

He looked at her. "Don't."

"Don't what?"

"If you've decided to come alive again, hallelujah. But don't come alive with me. I'm not the man for you to experiment on, Carrie. I'll be gone in two weeks, and you need someone who's going to be around for the long haul. You don't need to have your heart broken again."

She flinched, shocked. "What makes you think I've ever had my heart broken?" she demanded.

"Someone hurt you very badly. You don't want to make the same mistakes over and over again. You don't want to pick the same kind of man."

"You're completely different from Emerson," she said stubbornly.

"Am I? Maybe you just don't know me that well."

She put a hand on his arm, but he jerked away as if her touch burned him. "Don't," he said in a tight voice. "For God's sake, just *don't.*"

She stared at him, unable to keep the pain and misery from her face. "Sorry," she muttered. "It was stupid of me. I thought you wanted me."

The words were out now, shocking in their very simplicity. He shut his eyes for a moment, as if asking for help. "Of course I want you," he said roughly. "I'd be a fool not to. But you need love and cherishing. You need someone to father your babies and stay with you. All I can offer you is sex."

From somewhere she summoned a wry smile. "I'll take it," she said, moving toward him.

He didn't move, didn't dare move, simply because he wanted to so badly. "Carrie," he said, his voice deep with exasperation. "I'm warning you. For your own sake, leave me alone."

"Chicken," she said softly. And she reached for him.

Chapter Thirteen

Gabriel had a choice. He'd always had a choice, whether he'd known it or not. She stood in front of him, shy, trembling, filled with a misplaced love and longing. And he wanted her so badly he felt as if he were the one with the fever.

If he touched her, took her, his fate was sealed. There'd be no heaven for the likes of him.

He could move. Push past her and walk out of the house before he could change his mind. Or he could let her down gently, explain that he didn't really want her, that she should pay no attention to that bulge in his jeans.

He could do it, when there was nothing he wanted more than to take her. He could accept an eternity of longing for her, imagining what it might be like. He could punish himself, when it was more than he deserved.

But he couldn't do it to her.

If he walked away from her she'd never reach out again, he knew it with a despairing triumph. She wanted him, wanted him enough to fight for him, and if he turned her down she would never ask again. Leaving her would be just as cruel as taking her.

What was the saying, damned if you do, damned if you don't? He was damned, all right. He might as well enjoy his fate to the fullest.

He reached out and cupped her pale face, his long thumbs brushing against her trembling lips. "You're asking for trouble, Carrie," he said softly.

She smiled up at him, her eyes luminous in the shadows. "I know," she said.

He stared down at her, not saying a word. Maybe, just maybe it would work. She'd told him she'd settle for sex. Maybe if he made love to her it would be enough to make her realize that life was worth living. That if she found pleasure and warmth with him, she could find it with someone else, someone better.

Stupid rationalization, he mocked himself. He was grasping at straws, at some insane justification. Because he'd already gone too far. The moment his hands had touched her, there was no turning back. He was going to carry her up to the big bed beneath the eaves and make love to her, and if he spent eternity in hell for it, it would be worth it.

He put his lips against hers, lightly at first, feeling them tremble. Emerson MacVey had been good at sex—it was one of his coldhearted talents. Gabriel Falconi had never made love before, and each sensation was overwhelming, exquisite. The way her lips parted beneath the pressure from his mouth, the taste of her on his tongue, the soft, shaky little sigh she emitted when he kissed her ear. The thudding of her heart against his chest when he pulled her against him, pulled her arms up around his neck. The thudding that came from desire, and panic.

One last time his conscience surfaced, and he reached behind his neck and took her cold, trembling hands in his, holding her at arm's length. "Carrie," he said gently. "You don't really want to do this. You told me you weren't into one-night stands and casual sex."

"I lied. I've had dozens of men, Gabriel," she said, almost hiding her desperation. "I know when I want one. You're right about me, I have a saint complex. I need to take care of the world. But I don't need a relationship. I'm a big girl, I know when I have physical needs that need to be met."

Her lies were astounding. And the final straw. Anyone who could kiss with such innocent, untutored longing and lie with such fluency was more than he could resist.

"One night then," he said with a crooked grin. "One night of steamy sex, with no strings attached, is that it?"

"That's it," she said, with a calm expression on her face and desperation in her eyes.

He muttered something under his breath, something Augusta wouldn't approve of. And then, before he could change his mind, he scooped her up in his arms and started up the narrow stairs to the second floor.

He wasn't used to being strong. And she weighed too damned little. He needed to fatten her up, feed her pasta and cheesecake, cannoli and croissants. But most of all he needed to love her. For her sake.

And for his.

THE MOONLIGHT WAS COMING through the frosted windowpanes in her bedroom, and Gabriel didn't bother turning on the light. He set her down on the bed, and Carrie kept her arms around his neck, pulling him down with her, afraid he would change his mind once more.

At least she'd managed to convince him she knew what she wanted, even if she wasn't completely sure herself. For the first time in her life she wanted something just for her. She wanted Gabriel. And she wanted to feel alive again.

He could wipe out the memory of Emerson MacVey. He could make her forget her guilt. One night, that was all she asked out of life. Tomorrow she'd go back to good deeds and sainthood, to denying herself. For now she would take what she needed.

He covered her body with his long, muscular one, settling against her hips, and she could feel his arousal with a mixture of satisfaction and panic. He wouldn't leave her now. Not tonight. There was no turning back.

And then he kissed her, and her fear vanished. His lips were soft, damp, brushing against hers, teasing them apart, and then he used his tongue, tasting her, arousing her, so that the cool Minnesota bedroom began to fade away, and all that existed was the mattress beneath her and the wonder of his mouth.

He rolled to his side, taking her with him, his long legs tangled in hers, and his hands were sliding up underneath her cotton sweater, pulling it up. He broke the kiss long enough to pull it over her head, and she was lying there, skinny and cold, wearing only her plain white bra and baggy sweatpants, and she wondered whether he'd change his mind. He'd be used to gorgeous, voluptuous women, he'd be used to...

He put his mouth on her breast, through the plain white cotton, and she arched off the bed in shocked reaction. He moved swiftly, stripping off the rest of her clothes, and she was shivering, telling herself it was from the chill in the bedroom, knowing it was from something far more elemental.

He stretched out beside her, pulling her body against his fully clothed one, warming her, soothing her with his big hands. "I'm not going to hurt you, Carrie," he murmured in his slow, deep voice. "You can say no at any time."

She believed him. Her fear vanished instantly. "Yes," she said. And she put her mouth against his.

Her night with Emerson had been a blur of sex and wonder. This was different. Every touch, every taste was sharply delineated, etched in her mind. He moved his mouth across her collarbone, nipping, tracing a trail down to her breast, capturing the turgid peak and sucking at it. She made a quiet sound of intense pleasure, threading her hands through his thick, long hair, holding him there as his hands moved between her legs, touching her, with a feather-light touch that was reassuring, and then maddening, and then suddenly there, as she heard her voice choke on his name in the darkness.

He stripped off his clothes swiftly, efficiently, almost before she had a chance to come down, and then he was kneeling between her legs, huge and shadowy in the darkness, and her momentary panic returned as he cupped her hips and pressed against her. She was still trembling, sensitive from what he'd already given her, and she jerked back with a quiet shriek. But he touched her again, soothing her, and then she was ready, she was more than ready, she would die if she didn't have him, and she clutched at him, pulling him toward her, and he sank into her, inch by merciless inch, huge and hard and yet velvet soft.

She shifted on the bed to accommodate him, wrapping her legs around his hips, wondering if this was really going to work, when he finally sank into her fully, resting against her, his head cradled on her shoulder as they absorbed the sensations. She could feel herself rippling around him, and she wondered whether she could take much more. She'd had her pleasure—this was for him. A fair trade, and it was only slightly uncomfortable, and...

"Second thoughts, Carrie?" he whispered in her ear.

She shook her head, a complete lie. She owed him, she'd survive.

He pulled back, just slightly, and surged into her before she had a chance to prepare herself. And it was glorious. She moaned in the back of her throat, and her fingers dug into his shoulders instinctively.

"You weren't sure you were going to like that, were you?" he whispered, his voice low and sexy. "You were going to lie there like a martyr and suffer." He pushed into her again, and there was nothing saint-like about her gasp of pleasure.

He pulled her hands from his shoulders, pushed them down on the mattress and threaded his fingers through hers. "This isn't about pain, or guilt. This is about life." And he put his mouth against her, hot and wet and open, as his body thrust deeply into hers.

She shattered around him, instantly, shockingly, again, but he wasn't through with her yet. He knew how to prolong it, and he did, until she was sobbing, writhing, clutching at him, as he rocked against her over and over again. She was lost in some wild, crazy world of magic and dragons, sweat and desire and fulfillment that threatened to burn her to cinders, and it was endless, wondrous, an eternity that she never wanted to leave, when finally he went rigid in her arms, filling her completely, and she heard his voice, strangled, rasping in her ear. Calling her name across the white-clouded mists of time.

She wanted to hold him in her arms as he slept. She wanted to savor what had happened, relive every moment. But it had been too much, too overwhelming, and her body had its own kind of wisdom. Even as she fought it, it simply shut down, and she was fast asleep before he even lifted his head.

HE DIDN'T WANT to leave her. Didn't want to leave the hot, clinging warmth of her body, the frail yet strong cradle of her arms. He was ready for her again immediately, but he forced himself to pull away from her. She was sound asleep, her face shadowed with exhaustion and tears, and he wondered when she'd cried. If he'd made her cry.

He pulled the covers over them, wrapping her body tightly against his. There was no way he could ignore the fact that he wanted her again, and he had every intention of enjoying that need. It was part of life, a life that was going to be taken from him again far too soon, and he was going to savor everything until that happened.

He reached out and pushed her hair back from her tear-streaked face, and she murmured something in her sleep, nuzzling against his hand with age-old instinct. He could see the shadows beneath her eyes, and he considered calling himself every name in the book for taking advantage of her when she'd been weak and defenseless.

Except that he hadn't. Whatever the consequences, what they'd shared had been glorious, eternal. And if he had to spend that eternity in hell for it, it might just have been worth it.

He didn't sleep. He lay there in the moon-swept darkness, staring at the woman lying in his arms, drinking in the sight of her, shaken and shocked at the feelings burgeoning through the stranger's body he'd inherited, the one that now felt fully like his own.

He was in love with her. Emerson MacVey hadn't known how to love, but Gabriel Falconi did. Gabriel knew how to give his heart, even if it was a mortgaged one. One that had been nothing but a liability. As he lay there in the darkness, he considered the fanciful notion that if Emerson had ever once shared his heart it might not have exploded after thirty-two years. An interesting thought, but of no real importance in the scheme of things. Emerson was dead. It was up to Gabriel to salvage his soul.

He slipped out of bed just as the sun was rising, still achingly hard. She slept on, a faint smile on her face, and he covered her with the quilt, tucking it around her slender body before he left the room silently.

By the time she came downstairs, shy, sleepy, he'd managed to finish up the woodpile, stacking the logs in neat rows, enough for a long, cold winter. The wood stove was kicking out heat, the coffee was warm on the back burner, and he'd made muffins for her. Gabriel Falconi had unforeseen talents, including an aptitude for cooking. He just didn't have a gift for leaving well enough alone.

He fed her, keeping her mouth busy so that she wouldn't say what she wanted to say. He could see it in her eyes, and it terrified him. As long as she didn't say it, he was safe, he had a chance. Once she said it, he was doomed.

The house was banked against the winter, the windows caulked and tight. There was nothing more he could do, nothing that wouldn't be a major remodeling. Not that the place didn't need some solid work, but anything he started now would take months. And he'd be gone in less than two weeks. He had no reason to prolong being there except that he wanted to be with her, needed to be with her.

He fed her pasta and Italian bread for lunch, brownies and ice cream for dessert. He made her cappuccino, improvising with the limited kitchen equipment she'd inherited from her grandparents, watched her as she drank the cinnamony brew and ate every last bit of whipped cream. And when she started to say something, he leaned over and stopped her mouth, tasting the coffee and cinnamon.

When he went out to bring in more firewood she followed him, and just when he was expecting the worst, he ended up with a snowball smack in the middle of his chest. He'd responded appropriately, chasing after her, tossing her in the snow and rolling on top of her, until they were both frozen, breathless, laughing. And he'd kissed her again, and the snow began to melt beneath them, and he knew he wouldn't be able to keep from making love to her one last time.

They made it as far as the living room sofa. He stripped her snow-damp clothes off her as they went, leaving a trail through the kitchen. He kept her so busy she didn't realize that he wasn't letting her touch him, kiss him, caress him. He'd survive this if he could give to her, do for her. If he accepted anything in return he'd be doomed.

She was looking up at him, laughing, when they sank down onto the sofa, and then her laughter stilled as he filled her, thrusting deep, no longer afraid of hurting her. She arched up to meet him, her body tight around him, her arms clinging to him, her face pressed against his shoulder, and it was fierce, hot and fast, a firestorm of passion that was immediate and eternal, that left them both panting, sated, silent, with only the stillness of the winter afternoon around them, and the crackle of the wood stove breaking the quiet.

He held her, his eyes closed, unwilling, unready to face what he knew would come next, held her, knowing he had to let her go. If Augusta had thought to punish him, she couldn't have come up with a better torment. Even hell would pale compared to the thought of leaving Carrie.

And then he released her, surging to his feet and disappearing into the kitchen. He picked up the trail of clothes he'd pulled off her. He was still wearing his jeans, and he refastened them, rebuttoning his flannel shirt.

She lay curled up on the sofa, a secret, satisfied smile on her face. She looked up at him when he dropped her discarded clothes on top of her, and opened her mouth to tell him she loved him.

He stopped her. "I'll make some coffee," he said. "You stay put."

She smiled lazily. "Are you certain you don't have Scandinavian blood in you? You drink coffee like a Swede."

He had no idea what kind of blood he had in his veins. Whatever kind it was, it was only borrowed. He managed to return her smile, holding himself back from her when he wanted to pull her into his arms. "I used to drink tea."

It was her turn to look startled. "I knew a man who drank tea once," she said in a quiet voice.

Damn, and double damn. "Did you? Only one? I know it's a rare taste nowadays," he said, trying to get the right teasing note in his voice.

But she simply looked at him, confusion darkening her wide blue eyes. "Only one," she said. "Until you." And he knew she wasn't talking about a taste for Earl Grey.

It was already getting dark, the December afternoon closing down around them. He sat at the kitchen table, a mug of black coffee in his hand, and stared out into the twilight, trying to summon up the strength to leave her. He could hear her rummaging around in the living room, humming beneath her breath, a Christmas carol, and he told himself the dangerous moment over the tea had passed. There was no way she could connect him with the heartless bastard who'd destroyed her life.

She came into the kitchen, coming up behind him, threading her arms around his neck, pressing his head

back against her soft breasts, and he could barely sti-
fle a groan. He couldn't stop her this time. He couldn't
kiss her into silence, feed her into stillness.

"I love you," she said softly. "You know that, and
you've been terrified I was going to tell you. You've
been trying to shut me up all day, but it's really nothing to be afraid of." She kissed the side of his face, and
his eyes fluttered closed in sudden despair. "It's odd,
but it seems like I've always loved you. Even when I
was in love with someone else, it seems as if it was you.
Ridiculous, isn't it?"

He held himself stiff and still in the cradle of her
arms. "I thought you wanted uninvolved sex?" he
said in a harsh voice.

"I lied," she said simply, pressing her face against
his, following his sightless gaze out into the evening.
"I wanted you."

Damned. Damned to hell and back, and he knew it.
He'd earned it twice over in this lifetime and the last.
He'd taken a woman who was aching and vulnerable,
one who was ready to love. He'd taken her, and he was
going to abandon her, this time not by his choice but
by the cruelties of fate. He'd been given a chance to
save her, and he'd only brought her back to the same
vulnerable state he'd left her in the last time.

Damn him, he deserved it, he thought bitterly. He
deserved the torments of eternity. But she didn't.

He pulled out of her arms carefully, rising from the
table and looking at her. He had no choice in leaving
her, but he could choose when and how. He could stay
with her now, love her for the next two weeks, and
abandon her on Christmas Eve without a word of ex-
planation.

Or he could act like a bastard here and now, and make her realize she was well rid of him.

It was no choice at all. The second option would hurt him, start his punishment just a little bit early. It gave her a hope of salvation.

"I'd better be getting back," he said, his voice cool and distant. "Lars and Maggie will be wondering where I am. You're able to take care of yourself by now, aren't you?"

In the shadowy kitchen he could see the color drain from her face. She took a wary step back from him, searching for something to protect her, and he wanted to put his arms around her, to smooth the pain from her face.

Instead he reached for his coat, hanging on a peg near the door. "If you need anything just give Maggie a call," he said, shrugging into it.

"I'll do that," she said, her voice cool and lifeless.

He managed a jaunty smile. "And keep eating. You don't want to get run-down again. I won't be here next time you get pneumonia."

She flinched, so slightly another man might not have noticed. "No, you won't," she said evenly. "I haven't thanked you..."

"Consider me well rewarded," he said with a deliberate leer.

He might have pushed her too far. Her hands clenched, and he wondered if she was going to hit him. And what he'd do if she did.

She managed a faint smile. "Goodbye, Gabriel," she murmured.

It was worse than the heart attack that had exploded in his chest and ended up killing him. Worse than the paramedics beating on him, worse than the thought of an eternity roasting in the fires of hell.

And it was all he could do for her. "Goodbye, babe," he said, heading out into the frosty night air.

He didn't dare look back. If he saw her crying he wouldn't be able to stand it. Lars's truck started instantly with a low, throaty rumble, and he backed out her driveway, at the last minute glancing in the window. He could see her silhouette standing there, very still, very proud.

She'd make it, he told himself. She was tough, too tough to let a turkey like Emerson MacVey get to her twice in a lifetime. She'd survive.

Thank God, he wouldn't.

No one seemed surprised at his reappearance at the Swensen family home. Alexander Borodin had just left, and the place was in an uproar.

"A fortune, Gabriel," Lars boomed out. "The man has offered me a fortune."

"Beware of Greeks bearing gifts," Maggie said, unable to keep the light of hope out of her eyes.

"I thought he was Russian," Gabriel managed to drawl.

"He's an American, by God," Lars said. "Same as you and me."

"A very rich American," Nils piped up. "He's renovating a string of exclusive hotels all over the world, and he's offered Pop the job of redoing the woodwork. There's enough work to last into the year two thousand and beyond."

He'd blown it, Gabriel thought in sudden misery. It had all backfired. "You'll leave here, then?" he asked in a carefully neutral voice.

"Only to visit the sites. We need to set up a workshop right here in town, do most of the custom work here and then ship it to the hotels. I'd oversee the installation, but I've always liked the thought of a bit of travel. As long as I have Angel Falls to come home to."

"Sounds perfect," Gabriel said, disguising his relief. So he'd managed to do one thing right after all. He wondered how Augusta would stack that up against his seduction of Carrie.

"There's more than enough for you, as well, Gabriel," Maggie said. "Mr. Borodin saw some of your work, and he thinks you're very gifted. Almost as good as my Lars," she said proudly. "He wants you to help."

Gabriel shook his head. "I can't. I told you, I have a job just after Christmas."

"You don't know what kind of money this man is offering," Lars said. "It's unbelievable, it's magnificent, it's..."

"No more than you deserve," Maggie said sharply. "Can't you get out of your next job, Gabriel? Tell them something more important came up. Something with a future."

There was no future for him. He shook his head. "Sorry," he said. "I wish I could. But I'm committed."

"But..." Nils began.

"Leave the man alone," Lars said, looking at him closely, seeing him more clearly than Gabriel could have wished. "He knows there'll always be a place for him here. He'll always be needed. If he wants to, and he can, he'll be here."

"There are not quite two weeks till Christmas," Gabriel said. "I've finished out at Carrie's—at least I can help you get started."

"First of all, I need to find a place to work. We'll have enough to hire at least a dozen men, and I can think of twelve right now who need the work. The sooner we get going, the sooner those men will start bringing in some money," Lars said. And then his eyes narrowed. "You've finished at Currie's?"

"Finished," he said flatly. "What about the old mill? Is it still in working shape?"

"By heavens, you're right. Most of the equipment was sold off, but some of the really big stuff is still there, and the building's sound as a dollar."

"Not much of a recommendation," Gabriel said dryly.

"We'll check it out tomorrow. Now why didn't I think of that?" Lars demanded of the company. "There are times, Gabriel, when I think you must be my guardian angel."

"Not likely," he drawled. "Just someone passing through."

And outside the old house, the wind began to howl. And it sounded like the hounds of hell, calling to him.

Chapter Fourteen

Carrie stood in the darkened kitchen, watching him drive away, a sense of numb disbelief washing over her. She felt nothing but a vast sense of confusion. The pain would come later, she knew it. Once more she'd been a stupid fool, giving her heart to a man who had no interest in it.

For now she could bless the numbness that settled around her. She waited until the headlights disappeared into the gathering night, and then walked slowly back into the living room.

She stared at the sofa, at the rumpled cover and disarranged cushions. She stared at the wood box, filled with a fresh load of firewood, and she wrapped her arms around her body, shivering.

"Damn him," she said out loud, her voice clear and steady and very far from tears. "Damn his soul to hell."

The words shocked her. Suddenly, for some reason, they felt very real. Not a traditional curse without meaning, but a deliberate damning. No one deserved that, even someone who ran at the first sight of love.

"No," she said wearily. "Don't damn him. Just don't let me care."

She glanced around her living room, the rustic wood-paneled walls, the quilted wall-hangings, the snow-crusted windows. She hadn't done a thing to get ready for Christmas, and it was already nearly there. She needed to decorate her house, she needed to clean it, she needed good hard physical activity with no time to think, no time to brood. She needed to wipe the memory of Gabriel Falconi from her mind, from her body. She'd deal with it later, after he was gone.

She was usually far from compulsive about the state of the old farmhouse, but that night and the next day she would have done her Scandinavian grandmother proud. She scrubbed anything that held still, she put out candles and Christmas wreaths and hangings and fragrant boughs of fir, she even dragged in her own sizable Christmas tree, stuck it in a corner and decorated it with tiny white lights and all the quilted decorations she'd made over the year.

On the top of the tree she put the angel she'd made when she heard Emerson MacVey had died. It was a comical sort of angel, with a clownish face, an upturned grin and ineffably sad eyes. While he didn't look the slightest bit like the man she'd once loved, he'd always reminded her of MacVey. For some reason, he reminded her of Gabriel, as well.

She stepped back and surveyed the tree with a critical eye. Perhaps it was just the fact that she'd been fool enough to love two men who had no use for love, or for her. Or maybe there was something else, something she didn't quite understand, that linked the two men. Other than her own foolishness.

She heard the click-clacking of the freezing rain outside the window, slapping against the house. Inside, everything was cozy and warm, Christmassy, with the kitchen radio playing carols, the lights from the tree winking at her. Someone had brought her out a chicken pie among all the other goodies, and it was heating in the oven, sending wonderful smells throughout the house, mixing with the cinnamon potpourri she'd put in a bowl on the stove.

She was still recovering from her bout with pneumonia, she was exhausted from her compulsive housecleaning, and the weather report had gone from winter storm watch to winter storm warning, a full alert for those who understood such things. Carrie knew perfectly well she needed to curl up in front of the stove, eat her chicken pie, read something soothing, and make an early night of it.

She also knew she had no intention of doing so. Something was nagging at her, and all the housecleaning and decorating in the world couldn't drive it from her mind. She ought to give up on Gabriel, count him a lesson well learned, and go back to her solitary life, thanking God she'd been spared anything more painful. She kept trying to squash down her feelings, push herself back into a calm, martyred acceptance, when suddenly they burst forth in a great passionate rush, and along with them came knowledge.

He hadn't run away from her. He'd run away from himself. If he was a cool, heartless womanizer, he would have responded with an easy "I love you, too, babe." Instead, he'd frozen and then run, and she'd curled up like a wounded dog, ready to suffer in silence.

She wasn't ready to suffer any longer. She was going out on this dreadful icy night, and she was going to confront Gabriel Falconi. She was going to fight for him. And damn it, she was going to win.

GABRIEL STRAIGHTENED UP, stretching the kink in his spine, and let out a quiet, miserable groan. He'd spent the day in Lars's workshop, fussing over the details on a newel post, being so finicky that even the perfectionist Lars had teased him. Work wasn't driving her out of his mind. Nothing was.

He didn't want to be around anyone. The buoyant cheerfulness of the Swensen family, now that security was just around the corner, drove him mad. The silence of the house, when they were gone, was even worse.

He should have gone with them that night. The whole lot of them had piled into the pickup and the ancient station wagon and started on a caravan up to the old factory to check out its usefulness. Gabriel hadn't needed to go along with them to know it would suit them just fine. He'd done his part, saved his second victim, and everything was going to fall into place quite neatly, thank you. Besides, he didn't want to visit the scene of the crime. Even looking at the outside of the deserted factory brought a depressing wave of guilt over him.

He wondered how Carrie was doing. He told himself he was only concerned whether she counted as a success or not, and knew he was lying. Maggie had talked to her this morning, and even Gabriel's most careful questioning hadn't been able to elicit anything. Perhaps there was nothing to elicit. Augusta/

Gertrude hadn't come to the house, waving thunderbolts and threatening the wrath of God. Perhaps he was ready to concentrate on the third person he had to save.

Not that he had any choice in the matter. The longer he was around Carrie the more he botched things. The deeper he fell, in trouble, in love. He needed to forget his almost unbearable need to see her, he needed to leave bad enough alone.

He needed to find the third person whose life he'd ruined. He'd considered plain out asking Gertrude, but he already knew it would be a waste of time. She expected the worst from him, and she wasn't about to make things easier.

Maybe he ought to get out of town. Steve had finished with his pickup truck, and Gabriel had found he had enough money to pay him. If he got into the truck and started driving away from Angel Falls, maybe his third task would present itself.

He didn't think so. Lars and Carrie were no coincidence, neither was Augusta's presence or the name of the town. Christmas Eve was not much more than a week away. He had that long to find the third person, and then he'd be gone.

He knew where he was going, he'd accepted it. The other place, without question, was the price he had to pay for touching Carrie, for kissing her, for taking what she so sweetly, desperately offered.

And it was worth every moment of eternity.

He was still going to do his damnedest to find number three. Maybe he'd get time off for good behavior. Maybe if he did a good enough job with two of them, Augusta would overlook his failing grade with Carrie. Maybe he'd pass the test without the full extra credit.

Damn it, it wasn't fair! Other people died and didn't have to go through all this crap. Other people lived longer, they weren't cut off in their prime, when they had so much to live for.

And what did Emerson MacVey have to live for? Money. A cold, upscale apartment, a cold, upscale life. In his thirty-two years he'd done more harm than most people did in lives that lasted twice as long. It was just as well his had come to an abrupt end.

Hell, he didn't deserve to go to heaven. He accepted that, but he wasn't ready to give up. He'd find the last person and do his best. The one thing he wouldn't do was bring any more pain to Carrie Alexander. He wasn't going near her again.

The lights in the old kitchen flickered and went out, and Gabriel cursed in the darkness. It took him a few moments to find the matches and candles. In the darkness he could hear the freezing rain rattling against the windows, and he thought of the Swensens, out on such a night.

As if on cue, the phone rang. It took more than five rings for him to find it in the dark. "Gabriel, we're not getting home tonight," Lars boomed over the other end, jovial as ever. "The police have closed the main road, and the ice is murderous. Gertrude's going to put us up for the night."

All Gabriel's suspicions were instantly aroused. "Why Gertrude?" he asked.

"She lives right next to the factory," Lars said patiently. "You'll be all right there, won't you, boy? Don't go out in this stuff. You aren't used to it, and even for someone who knows what they're doing it's damned treacherous.''

"I'll stay put. The power's off."

Lars sighed. "It does that. I wish you'd come with us tonight.''

"And ended up spending the night at Gertrude's? No thank you. I'll enjoy being alone," he said. "If the lights come on I can get some more work done. Otherwise I'll just go to bed."

"You do that. Stay warm, Gabriel. We'll see you in the morning.''

Gabriel moved to the window, looking out into the darkness. The white stuff was coating the roads, the cars, the windows, making a little clicking sound. He stared outside for a moment, and then his eyes narrowed. Someone was driving down the road. Or more accurately, someone was sliding down the road, the headlights swinging wildly back and forth as they tried to control their vehicle.

They'd be fine, he told himself, trying to squash down his sudden panic. The street was relatively flat. If they just had enough sense to slide to a stop, to seek shelter, they wouldn't be hurt. And who in God's name was stupid enough to go out driving on a night like this?

He watched as the car drifted sideways. Even through the howl of the wind and the thickness of the storm windows, he heard the crunch as the front end of the car collided with one of the trees lining the road. He waited for the driver to move, to try to keep the car going. A moment later the headlights turned off, and the car disappeared into the swirling darkness.

It had parked three houses down, at the Milsoms' place. Someone obviously coming for the holidays, he told himself, staring bleakly out into the darkness. Someone who should have had the sense to wait for better weather.

But he knew he was fooling himself. Knew, as he heard the sound of her footsteps climbing up the snow-drifted front porch, knew as he heard her knock on the door, a loud, peremptory knock, knew who it was. He just wasn't sure why she'd come.

He considered not answering it, then dismissed it. As much as he didn't want to see her, he couldn't let her go out into the storm again. She was seven times a fool to have ventured out already. He wasn't about to let her risk her life again.

He was halfway to the door, the stub of a candle in his hand, when it opened. Hardly anyone in Angel Falls locked his or her doors, or even waited very long for a knock to be answered. She stood there, ice coating her hair, her coat, stood there in the open doorway looking at him.

There was no reproach in her pale, beautiful face. No despair, no longing, no heartbreak. There was simple, life-affirming fury.

She slammed the door behind her and advanced on him. "Who the hell do you think you are?" she demanded in a heated voice.

He didn't move. "Actually, that's a very good question," he said. "I'm not really sure."

"Don't give me that," she said, ripping off her coat with trembling fingers, and whether they trembled from rage or the cold he couldn't guess. Or something else, something even more elemental that was flowing between them, blazing between them, like a forest fire out of control. "You have no right to go to bed with me and then run away when I tell you I love you. No right." She dumped the coat onto Maggie's spotless floor and kept moving toward him.

"You told me you only wanted sex."

"I lied," she said flatly. "And you knew it."

He was backing away from her. Trying to stall, to give her one last chance to save herself. The fury was the best possible thing for her. He needed to feed that life-affirming fury. "Maybe I didn't care."

"Maybe," she said, still coming toward him in the darkened hallway of the Swensens' old house. "Or maybe you cared too much. I believe you when you say you have to leave. That you have no choice in the matter. I don't believe you when you say you don't care about me. You aren't a very good liar."

Emerson MacVey had been a consummate liar. Gabriel reached for that long-lost talent, for anything that would halt Carrie on her determined advance. He needed to convince her he was the worst thing that ever happened to her. Not for his sake—he'd accepted his punishment. For hers.

"Listen," he said, summoning a cool drawl as he ended up against the wall, no place to retreat to. "It's a simple matter of hormones. You were available, I was horny, we had a good time, as long as emotions didn't enter into it. As soon as they did, I figured it was time to leave. You aren't really in love with me. It's always the way with women—they have a good time in bed and then their puritan upbringing convinces them they have to call it love. They aren't allowed to simply enjoy their bodies. That's all it was, Carrie. Great sex. Believe me.''

He waited to see her fury fade, her face crumple into pained acceptance. She kept on advancing.

''It doesn't work, Gabriel. Try it again. Tell me it was lust that kept you by my side, spooning tea and soup down my throat, taking care of me.''

''Maybe it was guilt.''

That halted her, at least momentarily. ''Guilt?''

''You're an expert on that, aren't you? You blame yourself for everything bad that ever happened in this town. Just because some yuppie jerk closed the mill doesn't mean you're to blame. You were trying your best, but you were playing with fire. MacVey was out of your league from the very beginning, and you should have known it. You did your best, and it backfired. The mill was in trouble long before MacVey got his hands on it—it was just a matter of time.''

Her face was pale. ''How do you know his name was MacVey?''

Hell and damnation, he thought. ''Maggie said something,'' he improvised swiftly.

''Maggie doesn't know about him.'' Her voice was flat, accusing.

He could feel himself starting to sweat. ''Gertrude...''

''Gertrude doesn't know, either. I never told anyone about him. Not by name. Who are you, Gabriel? Why do I feel as if I know you?''

He opened his mouth to tell her, but the words wouldn't come. She deserved no less than the truth, but he couldn't give it to her. ''Lars,'' he said abruptly, the inspiration nothing short of a miracle.

"I never told Lars . . ."

"No, but you told me you were responsible for some coldhearted yuppie buying the factory and then closing it. And Lars knew the name of the man who'd done that. He's negotiating for the use of the building right now."

"He's not negotiating with MacVey."

"No," Gabriel said. "MacVey's dead. Burning in hell, most likely."

She stared up at him. "I don't think so," she said. "But we're not talking about MacVey. We're talking about you and me."

"There is no you and me."

"Guess again," she said. "Look at me and tell me that night we spent together was just a one-night stand. A roll in the hay. Tell me you don't feel something for me."

Damn. She looked brave and strong and alive, the fire of determination burning in her eyes. A woman like Carrie wasn't easily destroyed. A woman like Carrie was ready to fight for what she wanted. He'd warned her, and been damned for it. He could only go to hell once.

"I don't feel *something* for you," he said, his voice so flat and uncompromising that the light began to fade from her eyes. "I'm in love with you."

The expression on her face was worth it. She just looked at him, radiating joy and love, and the sight of her was so beautiful it hurt. He blew out the candle, plunging them into darkness, and pulled her into his arms.

Her mouth was cold, tasting of the winter air. Her body was trembling, and he knew now it had nothing

to do with the temperature and everything to do with
him. Too late, the words danced in the back of his
mind, and he shut them out, scooping her up in his
arms.

He made his way through the pitch darkness with
unerring instinct. Kissing her slowed him down, and
he had to kiss her. They stopped halfway up the flight
of stairs, and he let her body slide down against his.
She reached up and ripped his flannel shirt open, her
greedy hands running up his torso.

"Where are the Swensens?" she whispered, putting
her mouth against his chest, tasting him, licking him.

"Gone," he said, his voice strangled as her mouth
moved lower, to his stomach, her arms wrapped tight
around his waist. She was on her knees on the step
beside him, and she put her cheek against the fierce
swelling beneath his jeans, and he wondered whether
they'd make it to the tiny bedroom beneath the eaves,
or whether he was going to take her on the stairs.

They made it as far as the upstairs hallway. He
tripped on the frayed carpet, and the two of them fell.
She landed on top of him, soft, warm, fragrant, and
she found his mouth in the darkness, kissing him,
pushing the shirt from his shoulders, sliding her hands
down to unfasten his belt buckle.

This time her hands were sure, determined. This
time his hands were nervous, clumsy, as he stripped
the clothes from her, tossing them away in the darkness, pushing her down onto the worn strip of carpet-
ing, desperate to touch her, to kiss her, to have her.

He wanted to take his time, but she was as fevered
as he was. She pulled him up between her legs, and he

sank into her sleek, welcoming warmth with a muffled groan.

She arched up to meet him, wrapping her long dancer's legs around him, pulling him in deeper still, and her hands clutched his shoulders, her mouth met his with unerring instincts, and each thrust brought him closer and closer to heaven.

It was darkness, velvet darkness all around them. He cupped her face, kissing her eyelids, her cheekbones, her soft, wonderful mouth. He wanted to be gentle with her, to make it last, but he was hurtling along a dark path toward completion, and she was with him every step of the way, her breathing labored, her body slippery with sweat, her hands clutching him.

He felt her body tighten around him, heard her strangled cry, and then he was lost, thrusting into her, pushing them both over the edge into a star-tossed darkness unlike any he'd ever known.

He could still feel her body rippling, shimmering around him. He kissed her tear-streaked face, her nose, her mouth, and her lips reached up to kiss him back as she clung to him, shaky and breathless.

"You cry too much," he said in a low, tender voice.

"I haven't cried in two years. Not until you walked into my life." He started to pull away, and she clutched at him, suddenly desperate. "Don't," she said. "Don't feel guilty. People need to cry."

He'd never cried in his life. Doubtless another reason why his heart had exploded. "We need a bed," he said, lifting her into his arms, kicking the scattered clothes out of his way as he carried her the absurdly short distance to his bedroom.

The tiny room was very dark—only a fitful light came through the ice-coated window. He put her down onto the narrow iron bed with great care, lying beside her and pulling her into his arms. It was cold up there, and he flipped the heavy quilt over them, wrapping his body around hers.

"What do you think Lars and Maggie will say when they come back and find me here?" she whispered against his chest. "Do you think you'll be horse-whipped?"

"Congratulated is more likely," he said, threading his hands through her silky hair. "He and Maggie have been hardly subtle in their matchmaking efforts."

He could feel her smile in the darkness. "Neither has Gertrude."

Their bodies were entwined too closely for her to miss his start of shock, but luckily she jumped to her own conclusions. "That surprises you, doesn't it? It surprised me. I mean, she was my social studies teacher, for heaven's sake."

"How was she matchmaking?"

"She told me to go to bed with you."

Gabriel closed his eyes. Augusta's motives were beyond his comprehension. Perhaps she'd been stacking the deck against him. More likely giving him the hardest test of all, one he'd failed. One he was damned glad he failed.

"She did, did she?" he murmured. "She's smarter than she looks. Carrie, I..." His words were cut off as the sound of the telephone echoed through the house.

Both of them were very still, absurdly guilty. "Don't answer it," she whispered, clutching at his shoulders. "It's going to be trouble."

"I thought you liked trouble."

"Right now I don't like anything but you." The phone stopped ringing, and he began kissing her again, ready for her, knowing she was ready for him.

She was getting very bold, her hand reaching down to capture him, learn him, and he could barely control his groan of pleasure, wanting the world to center down on this narrow bed under the eaves and the woman beside him, the storms of life outside, the warmth of love inside. He kissed her mouth slowly, lingeringly, trailing his lips down her neck to the delineated collarbone, until he captured one nipple, suckling it deeply into his mouth, feeling her instant, fierce response that matched his own, and ...

The phone began to ring again. The world, intruding. Carrie was motionless, waiting. It was up to him, he knew it. She would shut out the world, and everyone in it, for him.

And he knew he couldn't do it. He'd spent thirty-two years thinking of nothing but his own needs and desires. Thirty-two selfish, dissatisfied years. He didn't want to bring Carrie to that same lonely spot.

"I have to answer it," he said, slowly disentangling himself, half-hoping she'd cling to him.

She let him go. "I know you do," she said, and even in the darkness he could see the love shining on her face.

He knocked over the telephone table in the hall as he tried to find it in the dark, and the panicked voice on the other end was that of a strange man.

"Lars, it's Martin Baker. I need your help," he said in the anguished voice of a frightened parent. "Something's happened to Jeffie."

And with a sudden, sinking feeling, Gabriel knew who the third person was. Somehow he'd ruined a seventeen-year-old kid's life. And it was up to him to save him.

Chapter Fifteen

"What's wrong?" Carrie sat up in bed, the quilt pulled around her, and with the fitful light from the frosted window she could see that he was in the midst of pulling on his clothes.

"I have to go out."

She scrambled from the bed, looking in the darkness for her own clothes. "What's happened?"

He didn't even pause. He seemed like a stranger, distant, determined. More like a saint than she had ever been.

"I have to find Jeffie."

"Who was that on the phone?"

"His father. He was looking for Lars. Apparently Jeffie's parents came home unexpectedly and found he'd been drinking. They had a huge row, and Jeffie took off in the car."

"Oh, God," Carrie said quietly. "I took him practice-driving once. He can barely manage to keep a car on the road in daylight, when the roads are clear and he's sober. He's going to be killed."

"No, he's not," Gabriel said flatly. "I'm going to find him."

"Why you?" She didn't know why she asked the question. Gabriel had seemed like the kind of man who shunned involvement. Risking his own life on icy roads for the sake of a drunken teenager should have seemed unexpected. Oddly enough, it wasn't at all.

"Why not me?" he countered. "His father can't do anything—Jeffie took their only car. Lars has a family depending on him. He shouldn't be risking his life out on a night like this."

"And you should?"

"I don't have that much to lose," he said. "I'll need to take your car."

"Fine," she said. "Where are my clothes?"

"What do you need your clothes for?"

"I'm coming with you, and I think it might be a bit chilly if I went outside naked."

"You're staying here."

"The hell I am. You don't know this area, I do. How do you expect to find a teenage boy on a night like this without a little help?"

"Carrie..."

"I'm coming with you. Now where the hell are my clothes?"

They were strewn from one end of the Swensens' house to the other. She found her jeans at the top of the stairs, her sweater halfway down the hall, her panties hung over the railing. She never did find her bra, and she could only hope they'd make it back there, in daylight, before the Swensens did. While Maggie and Lars might heartily approve of her being with Gabriel, they might draw the line at her underclothing decorating their house.

By the time she'd pulled her boots on and headed out into the ice storm, Gabriel was already at the car, and if she hadn't had the keys she knew he would have driven off without her. If she hadn't already discovered he was a better driver than she was she would have refused to give them to him, but as it was she simply buckled herself into the passenger seat and waited for him to pull out onto the ice-covered road.

He drove with maddening slowness, managing far more control than she'd been able to achieve. "Have you ever driven on ice before?" she asked, tucking her hands into her pockets to keep them from clenching.

"I don't remember."

"You have the strangest memory."

"Yes," he said, concentrating on the roads. The headlights speared through the icy darkness, and she could see his reflection from the dashboard lights. "Where should we start looking?"

"Your guess is as good as mine. I didn't see him on the road when I drove here, but I don't know how long he's been gone. For that matter, I don't know how long I've been with you tonight."

"Not long enough," he said, carefully navigating a turn.

"No," she said, "not long enough."

"I've got an idea," he murmured, and she had to admire his skill. Each time the car started drifting sideways he corrected it, keeping his speed careful, even. The sight of the salt truck was a blessed relief, the sight of the police car trailing it was less reassuring, particularly when the blue lights began to flash at the sight of Carrie's car.

"You'd better pull over," she said. "Jimmy likes to think he's Rambo."

The fresh salt on the road gave the cars slightly more purchase, and Gabriel slowed to a halt, grinding down the window of the car as the policeman shone a blinding light at them.

"Seen any sign of Jeffie?"

"How'd you know?" Carrie leaned across Gabriel, breathing in his scent, wishing to God they could have stayed curled up in his narrow little bed.

"His dad called me. We've got a couple of state police looking for him, but we didn't want to get too many people out on a night like this. Make things even worse than they already are. If I were you I'd go back and wait it out."

"All right," Gabriel said dutifully.

"Don't worry, we'll let you know when we find him."

Gabriel nodded, rolling up the window and edging the car forward. Carrie sat back and looked at him, trying to control the surge of disappointment. Disappointment that turned to a measured relief when he turned up toward the school, instead of back to the Swensens.

"I thought you said we were going home to wait it out," she said.

"It doesn't pay to argue with people like Jimmy. If you want I'll drop you off there, but I'm not going in till I find him."

"I'm staying with you. Jeffie needs all the friends he can get. I'd just as soon the police aren't the ones to catch up with him. His father won't have told them he was drinking, and Jeffie's going to have enough to handle without having to deal with the legal ramifications of drunk driving."

"It might be the best thing for him," Gabriel said. "Sooner or later you have to deal with the consequences of your actions."

"Are you talking about Jeffie? Or yourself?"

"I'm talking about everyone. What goes round, comes round," he said.

"Jeffie's already spent most of his life dealing with the consequences of other people's mistakes. His brother's and his parents' included."

There was a sudden, arrested look in his eyes. "Baker," he murmured. "What was his brother's name?"

"Lord, I don't know. Do you mean the name he was born with? Up until the time he dropped out of college and joined a commune, he was Clive Baker."

"Clive," Gabriel said in an odd voice. "Of course."

"What do you mean, of course? Did you know him?"

"No."

"Stupid question. Of course you didn't. Clive spent his life here, until he got accepted at Harvard. If it weren't for a bunch of sadistic preppies . . ."

"What do you mean?"

She shook with remembered fury. "A group of rich bullies decided to haze Clive, led by some cruel jerk. They teased him so badly he dropped out of school, went off to become one with the universe, and no one's seen him since. The Bakers gave up on both their sons then, I think. And Jeffie's been paying for it."

"And it was all the fault of some college buddies of Clive's?"

"No. But their leader was the catalyst for the disasters that followed."

"Do you think someone should be punished for being a catalyst?" he murmured, moving with a slow, steady speed up the long hill toward the union school. "Do you think they should be judged and found guilty, sentenced . . . ?"

"I don't know," she said. "It's not my place to judge people."

"No," he said in a hollow voice. "Nor mine."

The parking lot outside the sprawling school was dark and deserted, not even the streetlights glowing. The power outage seemed to have hit everywhere, and only in the distance could Carrie see the faint glow of lights. "He's not here," she said, unable to keep the panic and disappointment out of her voice.

"Yes, he is."

"Gabriel, there's no sign of him . . ."

"He's here," Gabriel said, letting the car slide to a halt. There was no sign of anyone in the vast ice-covered parking lot, but Gabriel unfastened his seat belt and climbed out anyway, leaving the car in neutral.

Without hesitation Carrie followed suit, barely able to stand upright on the glare ice. "Gabriel, he isn't . . ."

But he was already moving away from her, walking carefully with steady determination across the ice-covered surface. She followed his gaze in the glare of the headlights and saw what she'd missed before. The chain-link fence that surrounded the school property was down.

"Oh, God," she murmured, starting after him, but her feet went out from under her and she went sprawling, hard, on the ice. By the time she scrambled upright again, Gabriel had disappeared beyond the fence, heading down the steep hill.

She fell three times before she reached the fence, and she was half-afraid to look over the side, certain she'd see the Bakers' car a twisted mass of metal and broken flesh. Relief swamped her as she made out the shape of the sedan, still in one piece, resting against a grove of trees. The lights were off, but she could hear the radio playing, Christmas rap music, for God's sake, and she could see Gabriel leaning inside the driver's door.

"Is he all right?" she called, her voice shaking in the night air.

"He's fine," Gabriel called back, his voice rich with relief. "He's got a few cuts and bruises and he feels like hell, but he's fine."

"I'll bring the car closer."

By the time she'd edged the car along the icy surface Gabriel and Jeffie had appeared at the top of the hill. In the glare of the headlights Jeffie's face was pale, and there was a streak of blood across his cheekbone. He didn't look drunk or belligerent, he looked like a scared, lost little boy.

Gabriel bundled him into the back seat, then followed in beside him. "Drive to the hospital, Carrie."

"I thought you said he was all right?" She swallowed her sudden panic at the thought of having to navigate these roads again.

"He's taken some pills. He needs to have his stomach pumped, he needs to be checked out, and he needs to talk with someone. A professional. Can you manage it?"

"Yes," she said, because she had to.

"And turn on the radio, would you? Jeffie and I need to talk?"

It was maddening, it was terrifying, it was one of the hardest things she had ever had to do. She turned on the radio, finding something middle-of-the-road and innocuous, and began the endless slide to the hospital.

She wondered what they were saying back there in such low, serious voices. Was Gabriel giving him hell? Was Jeffie whining, or coming up with excuses?

Damn it, she wanted to be the one to lecture him, to take care of him, to make everything better. Letting someone else handle it was impossible, and good for her. She needed Gabriel around for more than the pleasure of his company. She needed him to prove that she wasn't indispensable. Someone else could be responsible for the state of the world. Responsible for one lost little boy she hadn't been able to help.

He took Jeffie into the emergency room while Carrie called his parents. When Gabriel finally emerged, he was alone, looking weary, sorrowful, like a man who'd looked into the face of hell and seen his own reflection.

"Is he all right?" she asked, rushing up to him, wanting to put her arms around him, afraid he wouldn't let her.

He pulled her tight against him, burying his face in her neck, and she clung to him, love flowing through her. "He'll be fine," he murmured. And then he lifted his head, looking past her.

The Bakers were coming toward them. Martin Baker looked more disturbed than she'd ever seen him, and Carolyn, usually the best-dressed woman in Angel Falls, wore one earring, ripped stockings, and her coat was buttoned awry. Her eyes were puffy with tears, and Martin's were suspiciously bright.

"Where is he?" Martin demanded. "Where's my boy?"

It's about time, Carrie wanted to snap at him, but she bit back the words. "He's in with a counselor," Gabriel answered for her. "He'll be released in a short while."

"I can't thank you enough," Carolyn began, her usually arch voice shaky with emotion. "When I think what might have happened . . ."

Gabriel just looked at her, and there was no judgment, no censure, only sorrow and understanding. "Life is too precious to throw away," he said. "Love is too precious to waste. Even for a moment." And putting his arms around Carrie's shoulder, he led her out of the hospital into the chill midnight air.

CARRIE DIDN'T SAY A WORD when they left the hospital, and for that Gabriel could be profoundly grateful. The past few hours had been the most harrowing of any lifetime. He could accept responsibility for a woman's broken heart and shattered life. He could accept responsibility for the economic collapse of an entire town. But the fate of one teenage boy was more than he could bear.

She simply fastened the seat belt around her, waiting for him to make the first move. When he tugged at her she went silently, willingly, resting her head on his lap as he made the long, slow drive back to the Swensens.

This time there was no tossing of clothes as they made their way upstairs. This time, when they made love, they did it in the narrow bed, sweetly, slowly, letting the pleasure stretch and grow, taking their time, savoring each other. And when they finished he looked down at her, cradling her head in his arms, and kissed her eyelids. "Carrie, I . . ."

"No," she whispered. "Don't say it. We have a little more than a week. Let's not talk about it. Let's just live it. No promises, no regrets."

And instead of telling her all the things he wanted to and couldn't, he told her with his lips and his body, arousing her all over again, until the night slid into daylight, and together they slept.

IT WAS A WEEK OF HEAVEN, and a week of hell. A week of lovemaking, cookie-making, a week spent feeding Carrie, body and soul. And a week spent feeding himself.

Two out of three ain't bad, he told himself, knowing Augusta wouldn't agree. Lars had already begun setting up shop in the old mill, Jeffie was going to AA meetings and family counseling and beginning to lose that sullen, haunted look. Only Carrie was going to suffer, and there was nothing he could do about it.

She steadfastly refused to talk about it. She knew he was leaving, knew nothing would change that. And yet she took each day, each hour, each minute with a delight that moved him, as well.

"Welcome, stranger," Lars greeted him when he walked into the kitchen. "It's Christmas Eve, my boy. You'll be coming to church with us, won't you?"

"Of course, he will," Maggie piped up, looking downright cheerful as she nursed the baby. "Carrie wouldn't let him miss it. And don't tease the man about making himself scarce. He's had better things to do."

"Am I complaining?" Lars said plaintively, his blue eyes twinkling. "He's been at the mill every day, and I can't imagine what I'd do without him. It's a rare gift you have, my boy."

He heard the words with numb despair. "It's Christmas Eve," he agreed. "And I have another job to go to."

The silence in the kitchen was palpable. "I thought you'd changed your mind about that," Maggie said softly.

Gabriel shook his head. "I'm afraid I'm committed. I just wanted to settle up my rent, and say goodbye."

"Don't be ridiculous!" Lars said gruffly. "It's me who owes you money, after all that hard work you've put in at the mill..."

Gabriel shook his head. "We agreed that would wait until you got your advance from Borodin. You can send it to me."

"But..."

"We agreed," Gabriel said sternly, counting out some money and dropping it onto the table. "And I'm a man of my word." He managed a faint grin. "Look at it this way, you'll still have time to get that train set Nils is longing for."

He was still good at manipulating people, he thought absently. That much of Emerson MacVey remained. The Swensens wouldn't accept the money for themselves, but they would for their children.

"My things are already in the car," he said. "I just wanted to say goodbye."

Lars looked shocked. "You can't be leaving already! No one expects you to be on a job site on Christmas Eve."

Gabriel's smile was wry. "You don't know my future boss. I'll miss you."

"You'll come back?"

He wondered whether he ought to lie. If he ended up where he expected, there'd be no way he'd ever see any of the Swensens again. They were good people—there'd be no question where they'd end up come Judgment Day. No sending the likes of them back for extra credit.

"If I can," he temporized.

"Have you already said goodbye to Carrie?" Maggie asked softly.

"I'm on my way there."

"She knows you're going?"

"She's always known I had to go," Gabriel said. "I never lied to her." At least, not in this lifetime.

Lars rose and shook his hand, and the Christmas cheer in his ruddy face had vanished. "We'll miss you, boy. Come back when you can."

"Is Gabriel leaving?" Nils wandered into the room, munching on a sugar cookie.

"Remember, he said he could only stay till Christmas," Maggie said.

"Oh, yeah," said Harald. "By the way, Gertrude told me to tell you she wants to see you. This afternoon. Four-thirty sharp."

He must have arrived in Minnesota around four-thirty, on Thanksgiving. It was such a short while ago, and yet it was a lifetime. He'd crammed more into those weeks than he had into his previous thirty-two years of living.

But he had no intention of going quietly to his doom, or trying to plead his case. Augusta had made up her mind long before he'd come back, she'd even conspired to make it harder for him. He wasn't going to make it easier for her. When she was ready to take him back she could damned well come and find him.

The roads were in decent shape—it hadn't snowed for several days, and the road crew had managed to clear up the mess from the ice storm. It was supposed to snow that night, a white Christmas, Carrie had said, managing to smile. He wouldn't be there to see it.

She was waiting for him. She'd dressed in something lively and red, and she was wearing jingle-bell earrings that rang when she turned her head. She was relentlessly, infuriatingly cheerful, handing him a mug of hazelnut coffee, chattering about the Christmas Eve service.

"I suppose you have to leave before then," she chattered onward, bustling around the kitchen.

"I suppose," he said, sitting and watching her, storing up the sight of her for the eternity to come.

"By the way, Gertrude called. She said to tell you she wants you to stop by on your way out of town."

"I got the message," he said lazily. "Are you going to keep running away from me or are you going to perch for a moment?"

She turned, startled, and gave him a wary smile. "I'll perch," she said, coming over and sitting on his lap, her arms around his neck. She was smiling very, very brightly, and he wanted to kiss that phony smile off her face. But somehow he knew she needed it. She needed the energy, the smile, the careless bravery. The only thing he could do was give it to her.

"I'm glad you're taking this so well," he said.

He heard the faint shudder of swallowed tears. "Of course I am," she said cheerfully. "I've always known you've had to leave. It's not as if you ever lied to me about it. I'll miss you, of course. But I expect that sooner or later you'll be back..."

"No."

The smile on her face faded for a moment. "No?"

"Damn it, Carrie, I told you...!"

"All right," she said firmly. "You won't be back. So I'll marry Steve, have half-a-dozen children who'll all be bald by the time they're twenty, and I'll think of you every Christmas Eve with a tear or two when I've had too much brandied eggnog. I'll be perfectly fine."

He rose, setting her on her feet, his hands lingering on her narrow waist. "I've already hurt you enough."

"Never," she said flatly. "Name one thing you've done."

He knew that he couldn't. Instead, he kissed her, long and deep and hard, kissed the lying smile off her face, kissed the brave eyelids that blinked back tears.

And then the bravery and tears vanished, and she began to sob deep shuddering tears that she cursed as she wept. "Pay no attention to me," she sobbed against his shoulder as he held her with tender hands. "I always cry at Christmastime. And I'll miss you— I'm allowed to say that, aren't I?"

"Of course," he murmured into her hair.

"Couldn't you lie to me?" She tilted her face up, and she looked very vulnerable, very sweet. "Tell me you'll try to get back to me? Even if you don't really want to, a little lie won't hurt you."

He looked at her, and the pain in his heart was worse than anything he'd ever endured. Massive cardiac arrest was a piece of cake compared to a simple, permanent break. "Damn it, Carrie..." he said.

"All right then, don't lie," she said. "Don't say anything at all." And her mouth stopped his protest.

He left her sleeping. She was curled up on the living room sofa, the bright red dress flowing around her, the salty path of her tears drying on her pale cheeks. It was four-thirty, but already pitch-black outside, and he knew there was no escape. He knelt down beside her, stroking her hair, touching her so lightly he knew she wouldn't awake. And then he rose, carrying the sight and the scent and the feel of her with him, into eternity.

He recognized the ancient Dodge Dart that squatted at the end of Carrie's driveway like a malevolent blue bug. His truck was still parked there, and he wondered what would happen if he got in, started it and tried to ram Gertrude. It was an idle thought, enough to summon a wry amusement from him, and he strolled down the long, winding driveway toward the waiting car.

"Get in," Gertrude said, rolling down the window.

He got in. He didn't bother with the seat belt—it wouldn't make much of a difference where he was going. "I must say, I wouldn't have thought it would be a GM product that would carry me across the river Styx."

"I'm glad you can still find something amusing about your situation, Mr. MacVey." There was no longer any sign of Gertrude in the old car. Augusta drove with her customary arrogance, and the slippery roads had no choice but to obey her.

He glanced out the window and realized they weren't driving on the roads. He leaned back against the seat with a weary sigh. "You've got your wish, Augusta. I did my best, and I failed."

"Indeed, Mr. MacVey."

"Don't call me that," he said mildly enough, determined not to let her get to him.

"Why not? It's your name. And there is no river Styx, and I am hardly Charon, the evil boatman. You're going back for the trial. I have my own opinion as to where you belong, and the answer might surprise you. But it's not my decision alone."

He glanced at her. She was glowing in the darkness, and he realized with a sense of shock that he was glowing, as well. "You mean there's hope for me?"

"Oh, there's always been hope for you," she said. "Mind your manners, and we'll see what happens."

CARRIE HEARD HIM LEAVE. She knew he didn't want her to say goodbye, so she'd pretended to be asleep, holding herself relaxed and still as his hand brushed her face, his lips brushed her eyelids.

She listened to his footsteps in the kitchen as he headed for the door, and she stuffed her fist into her mouth to keep from calling out to him. A moment later the rumble of a car, and he drove away, out of her life, forever.

She closed her eyes, absorbing the pain. She would survive. She always did, no matter what kind of mess she got herself into, no matter what kind of blows life dealt her. She wasn't sure if this current situation was her own fault, and she didn't really care. No matter how long she ached for him, hurt for him, waited for him, the days spent with him were worth it.

She was so tired. She'd been running on nervous energy, unwilling to rest while her time with him was so limited. That time was over now. She could close her eyes and let sleep come. Sweet, drugging sleep, where she could find Gabriel again in her dreams.

HE WAS WEARING his Italian wool suit once more, and his silk tie was too tight around his neck. He was glad the Waystation didn't come equipped with mirrors. He didn't want to look at his reflection and see Emerson MacVey's blandly handsome face. He'd had no choice but to leave Gabriel behind, a fallen angel. But that didn't mean he had to like it.

He sat alone in one of the waiting rooms, wrapped in that vast cocoon of nothingness. The smells were gone, he realized, the smells of Christmas. No cinnamon and hazelnut, no fir trees and gingerbread and hot chocolate. He was back in the void, and for a brief, savage moment he thought even hell would be preferable.

And then he wasn't alone. Augusta was there, tall, disdainful, staring down at him out of her cool blue eyes. "The decision has been made," she said.

He found he didn't want to hope. Heaven or hell made no difference to him at that point. Any place without Carrie was eternal torment.

"It's been determined that you tried very hard. To be sure, you wasted your miracles. One was for your own self, one was for a phone call, and you could have found Jeffie without divine intervention. Nevertheless, in two of the three cases you have done very well, indeed, and we're pleased with you."

He barely glanced at her. "What's the punch line?"

"You've broken Carrie Alexander's heart."

He stared down at his fingers as they idly drummed the arm of the chair. Short fingers, well manicured. Soft hands. "So? That's nothing new, is it? Apparently I'd already done so."

"I'm sorry, but she's in more trouble this time. Before she was simply suffering from an infatuation. This time she's not going to recover. Broken lives and broken bones mend. Broken hearts do not. She'll never marry, and she'll think of you every day of her life."

"Don't!" he said furiously, lunging to his feet. "She's too strong for that. She won't waste her life for a worthless bastard like me."

Augusta smiled. "She knows how to love, Mr. Falconi."

"Of course she does. It's not fair that she..." His voice trailed off as he realized he was looking down at Augusta. Augusta, who had stood eye to eye with Emerson MacVey. "What did you call me?"

"Why, your name, Mr. Falconi," she said. "You haven't earned your place in heaven, I'm afraid, so we have no choice but to send you to the other place. But you've been under a misapprehension. There is no such place as hell. The other place is life."

"Life?" He knew that deep voice. It was Gabriel's. It was his. He looked down at his hands. Large, graceful, scarred with the nicks and scratches that came from working with wood.

"Angel Falls, Minnesota. You're going back to Carrie, Mr. Falconi. You're being given a second chance. See that you get it right this time."

The blue light exploded in his eyes, and he was falling, falling, the pain sharp and cold and clear, and he wanted to scream, but when he tried, nothing came, and he reached out, and his hand came in contact with something solid. He took a deep, shuddering breath, deep into his lungs, and looked around him.

He was standing on Carrie's porch. The moon had risen, and a light snow was falling. He glanced up at the sky, and for one brief, mad moment he thought he could hear sleigh bells.

The house was still and quiet when he let himself inside. Carrie lay sleeping on the sofa, a quilt tossed over her, and as he glanced at the old grandfather clock he noticed in shock that it was one minute to midnight. He thought he'd been gone a matter of minutes. Or a matter of years.

The hand moved, the clock began to chime, a low, stately chime, and Carrie opened her eyes. She looked at him in wondering disbelief.

"You get me instead of coal in your stocking," he said, his voice hoarse.

"For how long?"

He thought back to the past few hours. It was distant, fading, like an old forties movie that he could hardly remember. It didn't matter. All that mattered was the future.

"Eternity," he said, reaching for her.

She came into his arms with her dancer's grace, and he lifted her high, holding her tightly. She was everything that had ever mattered to him, his heart and soul, his very life, and for a moment he just held her, absorbing her heat. And then he reached for the quilt, wrapped it around her, and he carried her through the house, out onto the icy porch, just as the clock finished striking midnight. In the distance they could hear the church bells ringing in Christmas, and he smiled at her.

"Merry Christmas, love," she said to him, her heart in her eyes.

And looking down at her, he knew he'd found his own heaven.

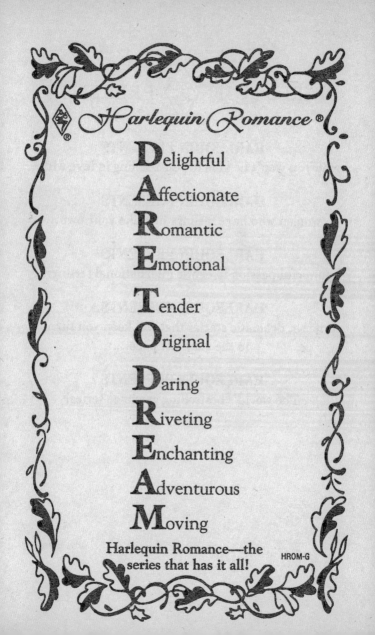

Harlequin Romance®

Delightful

Affectionate

Romantic

Emotional

Tender

Original

Daring

Riveting

Enchanting

Adventurous

Moving

Harlequin Romance—the
series that has it all!

HROM-G

HARLEQUIN PRESENTS®

HARLEQUIN PRESENTS
men you won't be able to resist falling in love with...

HARLEQUIN PRESENTS
women who have feelings just like your own...

HARLEQUIN PRESENTS
powerful passion in exotic international settings...

HARLEQUIN PRESENTS
intense, dramatic stories that will keep you turning
to the very last page...

HARLEQUIN PRESENTS
The world's bestselling romance series!

Harlequin® Historical

If you're a serious fan of historical romance,
then you're in luck!

Harlequin Historicals brings you
stories by bestselling authors, rising new stars
and talented first-timers.

Ruth Langan & Theresa Michaels
Mary McBride & Cheryl St. John
Margaret Moore & Merline Lovelace
Julie Tetel & Nina Beaumont
Susan Amarillas & Ana Seymour
Deborah Simmons & Linda Castle
Cassandra Austin & Emily French
Miranda Jarrett & Suzanne Barclay
DeLoras Scott & Laurie Grant…

You'll never run out of favorites.

Harlequin Historicals…they're too good to miss!

HH-GEN

What do women really want to know?

Trust the world's largest publisher of
women's fiction to tell you.

HARLEQUIN ULTIMATE GUIDES™

I CAN FIX THAT

A Guide For Women
Who Want To Do It Themselves

This is the only guide a self-reliant
woman will ever need to deal
with those pesky items that
break, wear out or just don't work
anymore. Chock-full of friendly
advice and straightforward,
step-by-step solutions to the
trials of everyday life in our
gadget-oriented world! So, don't
just sit there wondering how to
fix the VCR—run to your
nearest bookstore for your copy now!

Available this May, at your favorite retail outlet.

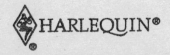

FIX